William Henry Withrow

Valeria, the Martyr of the Catacombs

A Tale of early Christian Life in Rome

William Henry Withrow

Valeria, the Martyr of the Catacombs
A Tale of early Christian Life in Rome

ISBN/EAN: 9783744743976

Printed in Europe, USA, Canada, Australia, Japan

Cover: Foto ©Andreas Hilbeck / pixelio.de

More available books at **www.hansebooks.com**

VALERIA,

THE MARTYR OF THE CATACOMBS.

𝔄 𝔗𝔞𝔩𝔢 𝔬𝔣 𝔈𝔞𝔯𝔩𝔶 ℭ𝔥𝔯𝔦𝔰𝔱𝔦𝔞𝔫 𝔏𝔦𝔣𝔢 𝔦𝔫 ℜ𝔬𝔪𝔢,

BY

W. H. WITHROW, D.D.,

Author of "The Catacombs of Rome and their Testimony Relative to Primitive Christianity," Etc.

"VALERIA SLEEPS IN PEACE."

TORONTO:

WILLIAM BRIGGS,

78 & 80 KING STREET EAST.

MONTREAL: C. W. COATES.
HALIFAX: S F. HUESTIS.

1882.

PREFACE.

THE writer having made the early Christian Catacombs a special study for several years, and his larger volume on that subject having been received with great favour in Great Britain, the United States, and Canada, has endeavoured in this story to give as popular an account as he could of early Christian life and character as illustrated by these interesting memorials of the primitive Church. He has been especially careful to maintain historical accuracy in all his statements of fact, and in the filling up of details he has endeavoured to preserve the historical "keeping" of the picture. Persons wishing to pursue the study of the Catacombs still further are referred to the Author's special work on that subject. See note at the end of this volume.

W. H. W.

TORONTO, *May 1st, 1882.*

CONTENTS.

VALERIA,

THE MARTYR OF THE CATACOMBS.

CHAPTER I.

THE APPIAN WAY.

"ENTRANCE TO A CATACOMB."

ON a bright spring morning in the year of out
Lord 303—it was in the "Ides of March,'
about the middle of the month, but the air was
balmy as that of June in our northern clime—
two note-worthy-looking men were riding along

the famous Appian Way, near the city of Rome.
The elder of the two, a man of large size and of
mighty thews and sinews, was mounted on a strong
and richly-caparisoned horse. He wore the armour
of a Roman centurion—a lorica or cuirass, made
of plates of bronze, fastened to a flexible body of
leather ; and cothurni, or a sort of laced boots.
reaching to mid-leg.   On his back hung his round
embossed shield ; by his side, in its sheath, his
short, straight sword, and on his head was a burnished helmet, with a sweeping horsehair crest.
His face was bronzed with the sun of many climes.
But when, for a moment, he removed his helmet
to cool his brow, one saw that his forehead was
high and white. His hair curled close to his head,
except where it was worn bare at his temples
by the chafing of his helmet, and was already
streaked with grey, although he looked not more
than five-and forty years of age. Yet the eagle
glance of his eye was undimmed, and his firm-set
muscles, the haughty expression of his countenance, and the high courage of his bearing, gave
evidence that his natural strength was not abated.

His companion contrasted strongly in every
respect. He had a slender, graceful figure, a
mobile and expressive face, a mouth of almost
feminine softness and beauty, dark and languish-
ing eyes, and long, flowing hair. He wore a
snowy toga, with a brilliant scarlet border of

what is still known as "Greek fret;" and over
this, fastened by a brooch at his throat, a flowing
cloak. On his head sat jauntily a soft felt hat,
not unlike those still worn by the Italian peas-
antry, and on his feet were low-laced shoes or
sandals. Instead of a sword, he wore at his side
a metal case for his reed-pen and for a scroll of
papyrus. He was in the bloom and beauty of
youth, apparently not more than twenty years
of age.

The elder of the two was the Roman officer
Flaccus Sertorius, a centurion of the 12th Legion,
returning with his Greek secretary, Isidorus, from
the town of Albano, about seventeen miles from
Rome, whither he had been sent on business of
state.

"This new edict of the Emperor's," remarked
Sertorius to his secretary, with an air of affable
condescension, " is likely to give us both work
enough to do before long."

" Your Excellency forgets," replied Isidorus,
with an obsequious inclination of the head, " that
your humble secretary has not the same means
of learning affairs of state as his noble master."

" Oh, you Greeks learn everything!" said the
centurion, with a rather contemptuous laugh.
" Trust you for that."

"We try to make ourselves useful to our
patrons," replied the young man, " and it seems

to be a sort of hereditary habit, for my Athenian ancestors were proverbial for seeking to know some new thing."

"Yes, new manners, new customs, new religions; why, your very name indicates your adherence to the new-fangled worship of Isis."

"I hold not altogether that way," replied the youth. "I belong rather to the eclectic school. My father, Apollodorus, was a priest of Phœbus, and named me, like himself, from the sungod, whom he worshipped; but I found the party of Isis fashionable at court, so I even changed my name and colours to the winning side. When one is at Rome, you know, he must do as the Romans do."

"Yes, like the degenerate Romans, who forsake the old gods, under whom the State was great and virtuous and strong," said the soldier, with an angry gesture. "The more gods, the worse the world becomes. But this new edict will make short work of some of them."

"With the Christians you mean," said the supple Greek. "A most pernicious sect, that deserve extermination with fire and sword."

"I know little about them," replied Sertorius, with a sneer, "save that they have increased prodigiously of late. Even in the army and the palace are those known to favour their obscene and contemptible doctrines."

" 'Tis whispered that even their sacred high-nesses the Empresses Prisca and Valeria are infected with their grovelling superstition," said the Greek secretary. "Certain it is, they seem to avoid being present at the public sacrifices, as they used to be. But the evil sect has its followers chiefly among the slaves and vile plebs of the poorest Transtiberine region of Rome."

"What do they worship, anyhow?" asked the centurion, with an air of languid curiosity. "They seem to have no temples, nor altars, nor sacrifices."

"They have dark and secret and abominable rites," replied the fawning Greek, eager to gratify the curiosity of his patron with popular slanders against the Christians. "'Tis said they worship a low-born peasant, who was crucified for sedition. Some say he had an ass's head,* but that, I doubt not, is a vulgar superstition; and one of our

---

* I have myself seen in the museum of the *Collegio Romano* at Rome, a rude caricature which had been scratched upon the wall of the barracks of Nero's palace, representing a man with an ass's head upon a cross, and beneath it the inscription, "*Alexomenos sebete Theon*," "Alexomenos worships his God." Evidently some Roman soldier had scratched this in an idle hour in derision of the worship of our Lord by his Christian fellow-soldier. Tertullian also refers to the same calumny; and Lucian, a pagan writer, speaks of our Lord as "a crucified impostor." It is almost impossible for

poets, the admirable Lucian, remarks that their doctrine was brought to Rome by a little hook-nosed Jew, named Paulus, who was beheaded by the divine Nero over yonder near the Ostian gate, beside the pyramid of Cestius, which you may see amongst the cypresses. They have many strange usages. Their funeral customs, especially, differ very widely from the Greek or Roman ones. They bury the body, with many mysterious rites, in vaults or chambers underground, instead of burning it on a funeral pyre. They are rank atheists, refusing to worship the gods, or even to throw so much as a grain of incense on their altar, or place a garland of flowers before their shrines, or even have their images in their houses. They are a morose, sullen, and dangerous people, and are said to hold hideous orgies at their secret assemblies underground, where they banquet on the body of a newly-slain child.* See yonder," he continued, pointing to a low-browed arch almost concealed by trees in a neighbouring gar-

us to conceive the contempt and detestation in which crucifixion was held by the Romans. It was a punishment reserved for the worst of felons, or the vilest of slaves.—ED.

* All these calumnies, and others still worse, are recorded by pagan writers concerning the early Christians. Their celebration of the Lord's Supper in the private meetings became the ground of the last-mentioned distorted accusation.—ED.

den, " is the entrance to one of their secret crypts,
where they gather to celebrate their abominable
rites, surrounded by the bones and ashes of the
dead. A vile and craven set of wretches; they
are not fit to live."

"They are not all cravens; to that I can bear
witness," interrupted Sertorius. " I knew a fellow
in my own company—Lannus was his name—
who, his comrades said, was a Christian. He
was the bravest and steadiest fellow in the legion;
—saved my life once in Libya;—rushed between
me and a lion, which sprang from a thicket as
I stopped to let my horse drink at a stream—
as it might be the Anio, there. The lion's fangs
met in his arm, but he never winced. He may
believe what he pleases for me. I like not this
blood-hound business of hunting down honest
men because they worship gods of their own.
But the Emperor's edict is written, as you may
say, with the point of a dagger—'The Christian
religion must everywhere be destroyed.'"

" And quite right, too, your Excellency," said
the soft-smiling Greek. "They are seditious
conspirators, the enemies of Cæsar and of Rome."

"A Roman soldier does not need to learn of
thee, hungry Greekling,"* exclaimed the centurion, haughtily, " what is his duty to his country!"

* " Graeculus esuriens," the term applied by Juvenal to
those foreign adventurers who sought to worm their way

"True, most noble sir," faltered the discomfited secretary, yet with a vindictive glance from his treacherous eyes. "Your Excellency is always right."

For a time they rode on in silence, the secretary falling obsequiously a little to the rear. It was now high noon, and the crowd and bustle on the Appian Way redoubled. This Queen of Roads* ran straight as an arrow up-hill and down from Rome to Capua and Brundisium, a distance of over three hundred miles. Though then nearly six hundred years old, it was as firm as the day it was laid, and after the lapse of fifteen hundred years more, during which "the Goth, the Christian, Time, War, Flood and Fire," have devastated the land, its firm lava pavement of broad basaltic slabs seems as enduring as ever. On every side rolled the undulating Campagna, now a scene of melancholy desolation, then cultivated like a garden, abounding in villas and mansions whose marble columns gleamed snowy white through the luxuriant foliage of their embosoming myrtle and laurel groves. On either side of the road were the stately tombs of Rome's mighty dead—her prætors, proconsuls, and sena-

into the employment and confidence of great Roman houses.

* *Regina Viarum*, as the Romans called it.

tors—some, like the mausoleum of Cæcilia Me-
tella,* rising like a solid fortress; others were
like little wayside altars, but all were surrounded
by an elegantly kept green sward, adorned with
parterres of flowers.   Their ruins now rise like
stranded wrecks above the sea of verdure of the
tomb-abounding plain.   On every side are tombs
—tombs above and tombs below—the graves of
contending races, the sepulchres of vanished generations.   Across the vast field of view stretched,
supported high in air on hundreds of arches, like
a Titan procession, the Marcian Aqueduct, erected
B.C. 146, which after two thousand years brings
to the city of Rome an abundant supply of the
purest water from the far distant Alban Mountains, which present to our gaze to-day the same
serrated outline and lovely play of colour that
delighted the eyes of Horace and Cicero.

As they drew nearer the gates of the city, it
became difficult to thread their way through the
throngs of eager travellers—gay lecticæ or silken-
curtained carriages and flashing chariots, conveying fashionable ladies and the gilded gallants
of the city to the elegant villas without the walls
—processions of consuls and proconsuls with

* It is a circular structure sixty-five feet in diameter,
built upon a square base of still larger size. After two
thousand years it still defies the gnawing tooth of
Time.

their guards, and crowds of peasants bringing in
the panniers of their patient donkeys fruits, vegetables, and even snow from the distant Soracte,
protected from the heat by a straw matting—
just as they do in Italy to-day.   The busy scene
is vividly described in the graphic lines of
Milton :

> " What conflux issuing forth or entering in ;
>   Prætors, proconsuls to their provinces
>   Hasting, or on return, in robes of state ;
>   Lictors and rods, the ensigns of their power,
>   Legions and cohorts, turms of horse and wings ;
>   Or embassies from regions far remote,
>   In various habits on the Appian Road."

CHAPTER II.

IN CÆSAR'S PALACE.

PASSING beneath the even then grim and hoary archway of the Porta Capena, or Capuan Gate, with the dripping aqueduct above it, the centurion and his secretary traversed rapidly the crowded streets of a fashionable suburb—now mere mouldering mounds of desolation—to the Imperial Palace on the Palatine Hill. This eminence, which is now a mass of crumbling ruins, honeycombed with galleries and subterranean corridors through what was once the stately apartments of the Lords of the World, where wandering tourists peer and explore and artists sketch the falling arch or fading fresco of the banquet halls and chambers of a long line of emperors, was then the scene of life and activity, of pomp and splendour. Marble courts and columned porticos stretched on in almost endless vistas, covering many acres of ground. Flashing fountains leaping sunward sparkled in the beams of noon-day, diffusing a coolness through the air, which was fragrant with blossoms of the orange and magnolia trees growing in the open courts. Snowy statuary gleamed amid the vivid foliage, and beneath the shadow of the frescoed corridors.

Having dismounted at the outer court and given their horses to obsequious grooms, Sertorius and the Greek repaired each to a marble bath to remove the stains of travel before entering the presence of the Emperor. Having made their toilet they advanced to the inner court. The guards who stood in burnished mail at the portal of the palace respectfully made way for the well-known imperial officer, but were about to obstruct the passage of the Greek secretary, when with a gesture of authority Sertorius bade the soldier to permit the man to pass.

"Quite right, Max, as a rule : but wrong this time. He accompanies me on business of state, before the Emperor."

Two lictors in white tunics with scarlet hem, and bearing each the fasces or bundle of rods bound with filets from the top of which projected a polished silver axe, came forward and conducted the centurion into the Imperial presence chamber, the secretary remaining in an ante-room.

The lictors draw aside a heavy gold-embroidered

curtain, and Sertorius stood in the presence of the Lord of the World, the man to whom divine honours had been ascribed, who held in his hand the lives of all his myriads of subjects, and the word of whose mouth uttering his despotic will might consign even the loftiest, without form or process of law, to degradation or death.

Let us note for a moment what manner of man this god on earth, this Diocletian, whose name is remembered with abhorrence and execration, the degenerate usurper of the august name of the Cæsars, may be. He sits in an ivory, purple-cushioned chair, near a table of inlaid precious woods. His short and obese figure is enswathed in the folds of an ample crimson-bordered toga, or fine linen vestment of flowing folds. His broad, coarse‾ features are of plebeian cast, for he had been originally a Dalmatian slave, or at least the son of a slave; but the long-continued exercise of despotic authority had given an imperious haughtiness to his bearing. He was now in his fifty-eighth year, but his features, coarsened and bloated by sensuality, gave him a much older aspect. He was dictating to a secretary who sat at the table writing with a reed pen on a parchment scroll, when the lictors, lowering their fasces and holding their hands above their eyes, as if to protect their dazzled eyes from the effulgence of the noonday sun, advanced into the apartment.

" May it please your divine Majesty," said one of the servile lictors, " the centurion whom you summoned to your presence awaits your Imperial pleasure."

"Most humbly at your Imperial Majesty's service," said Sertorius, coming forward with a profound inclination of his uncovered head. He had left his helmet and sword in the ante-chamber.

"Flaccus Sertorius, I have heard that thou art a brave and faithful soldier, skilled in affairs of State as well as in the art of war. I have need of such to carry out my purpose here in Rome. Vitalius, the scribe," he went on, with an allusive gesture toward the secretary, " is copying a decree to be promulgated to the utmost limits of the empire against the pestilent atheism of the accursed sect of Christians, who have spawned and multiplied like frogs throughout the realm. This execrable superstition must be everywhere destroyed and the worship of the gods revived.*

* Even as far west as Spain the following inscription has been found, which seems designed as a funeral monument of dead and buried Christianity : DIOCLETIAN. CÆS. AVG. SVPERSTITIONE CHRIST. VBIQ. DELETAET CVLTV, DEOR. PROPAGATO "—" To Diocletian, Cæsar Augustus, the Christian superstition being everywhere destroyed and the worship of the gods extended." But though apparently destroyed, Christianity, like its divine Author, instinct with immortality, rose triumphant over all its foes.

Even here in Rome the odious sect swarms
like vermin, and 'tis even said that the precincts
of this palace are not free. Now, purge me this
city as with a besom of wrath. Spare not young
or old, the lofty or the low; purge even this
palace, and look to it that thy own head be not
the forfeit if you fail. This seal shall be your
warrant;" and lashing himself into rage till the
purple veins stood out like whipcords on his
forehead, he tossed his signet ring across the
table to the scribe, who prepared a legal instrument to which he affixed the Imperial seal.

"May it please your Imperial Majesty," said
the centurion, with an obeisance, "I am a rude
soldier, unskilled to speak in the Imperial presence; but I have fought your Majesty's enemies
in Iberia, in Gaul, in Dacia, in Pannonia, and
in Libya, and am ready to fight them anywhere.
Nevertheless, I would fain be discharged from
this office of censor of the city. I know naught,
save by Rumour, who is ever a lying jade, your
Imperial Majesty, against this outlawed sect.
And I know some of them who were brave
soldiers in your Imperial Majesty's service, and
many others are feeble old men or innocent
women and children. I pray you send me rather
to fight against the barbarian Dacians than
against these."

"I was well informed then that you were a

bold fellow," exclaimed the Emperor, his brow flushing in his anger a deeper hue; "but I have need of such. Do thy duty, on thy allegiance, and see that thou soon bring these culprits to justice. Is it not enough that universal rumour condemns them? They are pestilent sedition-mongers, and enemies of the gods and of the State."

"I, too, am a worshipper of the gods," continued the intrepid soldier, "and will fail not to keep my allegiance to your Imperial Majesty, to the State, and to those higher powers," and he walked backward out of the Imperial presence. As he rejoined his secretary a cloud sat on his brow. He was moody and taciturn, and evidently little pleased with his newly-imposed duties. But the confirmed habit of unquestioning obedience inherent in a Roman soldier led to an almost mechanical acceptance of his uncongenial task. Emerging from the outer court he proceeded to his own house, in the populous region of the Aventine Hill, now a deserted waste, covered with kitchen gardens and vineyards. In the meantime we turn to another part of the great Imperial palace.

CHAPTER III.

EMPRESS AND SLAVE.

USING the time-honoured privilege of ubiquity accorded to imaginative writers, we beg to conduct our readers to a part of the stately palace of Diocletian, where, if they had really been found in their own proper persons, it would have been at the peril of their lives. After fifteen long centuries have passed, we may explore without let or hindrance the most private apartments of the once all-potent masters of the world. We may roam through their unroofed banquet-chambers. We may gaze upon the frescoes, carvings, and mosaics which met their eyes. We may behold the evidences of their luxury and profligacy. We may thread the secret corridors and galleries connecting the chambers of the palace—all now open to the light of day.

We may even penetrate to the boudoirs and
tiring rooms of the proud dames of antiquity.
We may even examine at our will the secrets of
the toilet—the rouge pots and vases for cosmetics
and unguents, the silver mirrors, fibulæ or
brooches, armlets and jewels, and can thus reconstruct much of that old Roman life which has
vanished forever from the face of the earth.*

By the light of modern exploration and discovery, therefore, we may enter the private apartments of ladies of the Imperial household, and
in imagination re-furnish these now desolate and
ruinous chambers with all the luxury and magnificence of their former prime. A room of com-
modious size is paved with tesselated marble
slabs, adorned with borders and designs of brilliant mosaic. The walls are also marble, save
where an elegant fresco on a stucco ground—
flowers or fruit or graceful landscape†—greet the

* On the Palatine Hill may still be seen, in the palace
of the Flavii, the frescoed private apartments and banquet-chambers of the emperors—in the walls are even
the lead water-pipes, stamped with the maker's name ;
and the innumerable ancient relics in the museums of
Rome and Naples give such an insight as nothing else
can impart of the life and character of the palmy days
of the empire.

† On the banquet-room mentioned in the last note are
some remarkable frescoes, among other objects being
glass vases through whose transparent sides are seen

eye. A small fountain throws up its silver spray, imparting a grateful coolness to the air. Windows, void of glass, but mantled and screened by climbing plants and rare exotics, look out into a garden where snowy marble statues are relieved against the dark green of the cypress and ilex. Around the room are busts and effigies of the Imperial household 'or of historical characters. There is, however, a conspicuous absence of the mythological figures, whose exquisite execution does not atone for their sensuous conception, which, rescued from the *debris* of ancient civilization, crowd all the Art-galleries of Europe. That this is not the result of accident but of design is seen by an occasional empty pedestal or niche.. Distributed at intervals are couches and tables of costly woods, inlaid with ivory, and bronze and silver candelabra, lamps and other household objects of ornament or use. Sitting in an ivory chair amid all this elegance and luxury was a lady in the very flower of her youth, of queenly dignity and majestic beauty. She wore a snowy *stola*, or robe of finest linen, with purple border, flowing in ample folds to her sandaled feet. Over this was negligently thrown a saffron-coloured veil of thinnest tissue. She held in her hand a burnished silver mirror, at which she

exquisitely painted fruits—as fresh, apparently, after eighteen centuries as if executed within a few months. -

glanced carelessly from time to time, while a comely slave with dark lustrous eyes and finely-formed features carefully brushed and braided her long and rippling hair.

This queenly presence was the young and lovely Empress Valeria, the daughter of Diocletian and Prisca, and wife of the co-Emperor, Galerius Cæsar. The object of envy of all the women of Rome, she lived to become within a few short years the object of their profoundest commiseration. Of her even the unsympathetic Gibbon remarks that "her melancholy adventures might furnish a very singular subject for tragedy."

"Nay, now, Callirhoë," said the Empress, with a weary smile, "that will do! Put up my hair and bind it with this fillet," and she held out a gold-embroidered ribband. "Thou knowest I care not for the elaborate coiffure that is now so fashionable."

"Your Majesty needs it not," said the slave, speaking Greek with a low sweet voice, and with an Attic purity of accent. "As one of your own poets has said, you appear 'when unadorned, adorned the most.'"

"Flatterer," said the Empress, tapping her gaily and almost caressingly with a plumy fan of ostrich feathers which she held lightly in one hand, "you are trying to spoil me."

"Such goodness as thine, sweet mistress," said the slave, affectionately kissing her hand, "it would be impossible to spoil."

"Dost know, Callirhoë," said the young Empress, with a smile of bewitching sweetness, "that I have a surprise for thee? It is, thou knowest, my birthday, and in my honour is the banquet given to-day. But I have a greater pleasure than the banquet can bestow. I give thee this day thy freedom. Thou art no more a slave, but the freedwoman of the Empress Valeria. See, here are the papers of thy manumission," and she drew from the girdle of her robe a sealed and folded parchment, which she handed to the now emancipated slave.

"Dearest mistress!" exclaimed the faithful creature, who had thrown herself on the marble pavement and was kissing the sandaled feet of the beautiful Empress, but an outburst of sobs and tears choked her utterance.

"What! weeping!" exclaimed Valeria. "Are you sorry then?"

"Nay, they are tears of joy," exclaimed the girl, smiling through her tears, like the sun shining through a shower; "not that I tire of thy service; I wish never to leave it. But I rejoice that my father's daughter can serve thee no longer as thy slave, but as thy freedwoman."

"I should indeed be sorry to lose thee," said

the august lady with a wistful smile. "If I thought I should, I would almost regret thy manumission; for believe me, Callirhoë, I have need of true friends, and thou, I think, wilt be a faithful one."

"What! I, but this moment a poor slave, the friend of the fairest and most envied lady in all Rome! Nay, now thou laughest at me; but believe me I am still heart and soul and body thy most devoted servant."

"I do believe it, child," said the Empress; "but tell me, pray, why thou speakest in that proud melancholy tone of thy father? Was he a freedman?"

"Nay, your Majesty, he was free-born; neither he nor his fathers were ever in bondage to any man,"—and the fair face of the girl was suffused with the glow of honest pride in the freeborn blood that flowed in her veins.

"Forgive me, child, if I touched a sore spot in thy memory. Perchance I may heal it. Money can do much, men say."

"In this case, dearest mistress, it is powerless. But from thee I can have no secrets, if you care to listen to the story of one so long a slave."

"I never knew thou wert aught else, child. My steward bought thee in the slave market in the Suburra. Tell me all."

"'Tis a short story, but a sad one, your

Majesty," said the girl, as she went on braiding her mistress's hair. "My father was a Hebrew merchant, a dealer in precious stones, well esteemed in his nation. He lived in Damascus, where I was born. He named me after the beautiful fountain near the Jordan of his native land."

"I thought it had been from the pagan goddess," interrupted the Empress.

"Nay, 'twas from the healing fountain of Callirhoë, in Judæa," continued the girl. "When my mother died, my father was plunged into inconsolable grief, and fell ill, well-nigh to death. The most skilled physician in Damascus, Eliezer by name, brought him back to life; but his friends thought he had better let him die, for he converted him to the hated Christian faith. Persecuted by his kinsmen, he came to Antioch with my brother and myself, that he might join the great and flourishing Christian Church in that city.* While on a trading voyage to Smyrna, in which we children accompanied our father, we were captured by Illyrian pirates, and carried to the slave market at Ravenna. There I was purchased by a slave dealer from Rome, and my father and brother were sold I know not whither.

* Shortly after this time, that Church numbered 100,000 persons.

I never saw them again,"—and she heaved a weary and hopeless sigh.

"Poor child!" said the Empress, a tear of sympathy glistening on her cheek, "I fear that I can give thee little help. 'Tis strange how my heart went out toward thee when thou wert first brought so tristful and forlorn into my presence. 'Tis a sad world, and even the Emperors can do little to set it right."

"There is One who rules on high, dear lady, the God of our fathers, by whom kings rule and princes decree judgment. He doeth all things well."

"Yes, child, I am not ignorant of the God of the Jews and Christians. What a pity that there should be such bitter hate on the part of your countrymen towards those who worship the same great God."

"Yes," said Callirhoë, "blindness in part hath happened to Israel. If they but knew how Jesus of Nazareth fulfils all the types and prophecies of their own Scriptures, they would hail Him as the true Messiah of whom Moses and the prophets did write."

"Well, child, I will help thee to find thy father, if possible, though I fear it will be a difficult task. Ask me freely anything that I can do. As my freedwoman, you will, of course, bear my name with your own. Now send my slave Juba to accompany me to the banquet-hall."

Callirhoë, or as we may now call her, after the Roman usage, Valeria Callirhoë, fervently kissed the outstretched hand of her august mistress and gracefully retired.

It may excite some surprise to find such generous sentiments and such gentle manners as we have described attributed to the daughter of a persecuting Emperor and the wife of a stern Roman general. But reasons are not wanting to justify this delineation. Both Valeria and her mother Prisca, during their long residence at Nicomedia, where the Emperor Diocletian had established his court, became instructed in the Christian religion by the bishop of that important see. Indeed, Eusebius informs us that among them there were many Christian converts, both Prisca and Valeria, in the Imperial palace. Diocletian and his truculent son-in-law, Galerius, were bigoted pagans, and the mother of the latter was a fanatical worshipper of the goddess Cybele. The spread of Christianity even within the precincts of the palace provoked her implacable resentment, and she urged on her son to active persecution. A council was therefore held in the palace at Nicomedia, a joint edict for the extirpation of Christianity was decreed, and the magnificent Christian basilica was razed to the ground. The very next day the edict was torn from the public forum by an indignant Christian, and the Imperial palace was almost entirely destroyed by fire. The origin of this disaster is unknown, but it was ascribed to the Christians, and intensified the virulence of the persecution. Diocletian proceeded to Rome to celebrate a military triumph and to concert with his western colleagues more vigorous methods of persecution. It is at this period that the opening scenes of our story take place.

CHAPTER IV.

THE IMPERIAL BANQUET.

AT the summons of Callirhoë a Nubian female slave, Juba by name, an old family nurse, skilled in the use of herbs and potions, made her appearance. Her huge and snowy turban and her bright-coloured dress strikingly contrasted with her jet complexion and homely features. Yet, as the personal attendant of the young empress, it was her duty to accompany her mistress to the banquet-hall, to stand behind her chair, to adjust her robes, hold her fan, and obey her every word or gesture. As she drew aside the curtain of the apartment which shut out the light and heat, two lictors who guarded the door sprang to their feet and preceded the empress through the marble corridor to the *triclinium*, or banquet chamber. It was a family party, rather

than a state banquet, but neither Greeks nor
Romans practised a profuse hospitality nor held
large social or festive gatherings like those of
modern times. Their feasts were rather for the
intense epicurean pleasure of a favoured few than
for the rational enjoyment of a larger company.*

Couches inlaid with ivory and decked with
cushions surrounded three sides of a hollow
square. On these the emperor and his male
guests reclined, each resting on his left arm.
On ivory chairs facing the open side of the
square sat the Empress Prisca (a majestic-look-
ing matron of somewhat grave aspect), Valeria,
and a lady of the court, each accompanied by
her female slave. The extreme ugliness of the
Nubian Juba acted as a foil for the striking
beauty of Valeria.

First of all, the guests were crowned with
wreaths of fair and fragrant flowers. Then
elegantly dressed slaves brought in, to the sound
of music, the different courses: first eggs dressed
with vinegar, olives and lettuce, like our salad;
then roast pheasants, peacocks' tongues and
thrushes, and the livers of capons steeped in
milk; next oysters brought alive from the dis-

* On a single supper for his friends, Lucullus, who is
said to have ted his lampreys with the bodies of his
slaves, is recorded to have expended 50,000 denarii—
about $8,500.

t int shores of Great Britain, and, reversing our order, fish in great variety—one of the most beautiful of these was the purple mullet—served with high-seasoned condiments and sauces. Of solid meats the favourite dish was a roast sucking pig, elegantly garnished. Of vegetables they had nothing corresponding to our potatoes, but, instead, a profusion of mallows, lentils, truffles, and mushrooms. The banquet wound up with figs, olives, almonds, grapes, tarts and confections, and apples—hence the phrase *ab ovo ad mala*.

After the first course the emperor poured out a libation of Falernian wine, with the Greek formula, " to the supreme God," watching eagerly if his wife and daughter would do the same. Lacking the courage to make a bold confession of Christianity, and thinking, with a casuistry that we shall not attempt to defend, that the ambiguity of the expression excused the act, they also, apparently to the great relief of the emperor, poured out a libation and sipped a small quantity of the wine. The emperor then drank to the health of his wife and daughter, wishing the latter many returns of the auspicious day they had met to celebrate. Each of the guests also made, according to his ability, a complimentary speech, which the ladies acknowledged by a gracious salutation. After the repast slaves brought perfumed water and embroidered nap-

kins for the guests to wash their fingers, which
had been largely employed in the process of dining.

The most of the guests were sycophants and
satellites of the emperor, and in the intervals
between the courses employed their art in
flattering his vanity or fomenting his prejudices.
One of them, Semphronius by name, an old
fellow with a very bald and shiny head and a
very vivacious manner, made great pretensions
to the character of a philosopher or professor of
universal knowledge, and was ever ready, with a
great flow of often unmeaning words, to give a
theory or explanation of every conceivable subject. Others were coarse and sensual-looking
bon vivants, who gave their attention chiefly to
the enjoyment of the good fare set before them.
Another sinister-looking fellow, with a disagree-
able cast in one eye and a nervous habit of
clenching his hand as if grasping his sword, was
Quintus Naso, the prefect of the city. He had
been a successful soldier, or rather butcher, in
the Pannonian wars, and was promoted to his
bad eminence of office on account of his truculent
severity. Of very different character, however,
was a young man of noble family, Adauctus by
name, who was present in his official character
as Treasurer of the Imperial Exchequer.* He

* His name and office are recorded even by so skep-
tical a critic as Gibbon, and his epitaph has been found
in the Catacombs. See Withrow's Catacombs, p. 46.

almost alone of the guests paid a courteous attention to the high-born ladies of the party, to whom he frequently addressed polite remarks while the others were intent only in fawning on the great source of power. He, also, alone of all present, conspicuously refrained from pouring out a libation—a circumstance which did not escape the keen eye of the emperor. After interrupted talk on general topics, in which the ladies took part, the conversation drifted to public matters, on which they, were not expected to meddle.

"Well, Naso, how was the edict received?" said the emperor to the prefect, as a splendid roast peacock, with sadly despoiled plumage, was removed.

"As every command of your divine Majesty should be received," replied Naso, "with respectful obedience. One rash fool, indeed, attempted to tear it down from the rostra of the Forum, like that mad wretch at Nicomedia; but he was taken in the act. He expiates to-night his crime, so soon as I shall have wrung from him the names of his fanatical accomplices,"—and he clenched his hands nervously, as though he were himself applying the instruments of torture.

"And you know well how to do that," said the emperor with a sneer, for, like all tyrants, he despised and hated the instruments of his tyranny.

"You may well call them fanatics, good Naso,"

chimed in the would-be philosopher, Semphronius; "a greater set of madmen the world never saw. They believe that this Chrestus whom they worship actually rose from the dead. Heard ever any man such utter folly as that! Whereas I have satisfied myself, from a study of the official records, that he was only a Jewish thaumaturge and conjuror, who used to work pretended miracles by means of dupes and accomplices. And when, for his sedition, he was put to death as the vilest of felons, these accomplices stole his body and gave out that he rose from the dead." *

"I have heard," said Adauctus gravely, "that the Romans took care to prevent such a trick as that by placing a maniple of soldiers on guard at His grave."

"Yes, I believe they say so," went on the unabashed Semphronius; "but if they did, the dastards were either overpowered, or they all fell asleep while his fellow-knaves stole his body away."

"Come now, Semphronius," said the emperor, "that is too improbable a story about a whole maniple of soldiers. You and I know too well, Naso, the Roman discipline to accept such an absurd story as that."

* Strauss and Renan and their rationalizing school rival this pagan sophist in eliminating the miraculous from the sacred record.

"Oh, if your divine Majesty thinks it improbable, I fully admit that it is so," the supple sophist eagerly replied. "I am inclined to identify this impostor and a kinsman of his who was beheaded by the divine Herod with the Janus and Jambres whose story is told in the sacred books of the Jews. But it is evident, from the identity of name of one of these with the god Janus, that they merely borrowed the story from the Roman mythology. This execrable superstition, they say, was brought to Rome by two brothers named Paulus and Simon Magus. They both expiated their crimes, one in the Mammertine Prison, the other without the Ostian Gate. They say also that when Simon the magician struck the prison wall, a well of water gushed forth for some of their mystic rites; and that when the head of Paulus was smitten off it bounded three times on the ground, and at each spot where it touched a well of water sprang up. But these are stories that no sane man can believe."*

"I quite agree with you in that," said Adauctus.

"Do you, indeed?" exclaimed the Emperor; "I am glad to know that so brave and trusted an officer can say so."

* Yet these stories, too incredible for this old pagan, were gravely related to the present writer, on the scene of the alleged miracles, by the credulous Romans of to-day.

"I believe, your Majesty, that half the stories told about the Christians are calumnies that no candid man can receive," continued the young officer.

"You are a bold man to say so, for they have few friends and many enemies at court," replied Diocletian; "but we will soon extort their secrets by this edict. Will we not, good Naso?"

"It will not be my fault if we do not, your divine Majesty," replied that worthy, with a more hideous leer than usual in his cruel eye.

"Another thing these fools of Christians believe," interjected the garrulous philosopher, "is, that when they die their souls shall live in some blander clime, and breathe some more ethereal air. 'Tis this that makes them seem to covet martyrdom, as they call it, instead of, like all sane men, shunning death."

"But do not your own poets," chimed in the soft voice of Valeria, "speak of the Elysian fields and the asphodel meadows where the spirits of heroes walk, and of the bark of Charon, who ferries them across the fatal Styx?"

"True, your most august Highness," replied the pedant with grimace intended to be polite, "but those fables are intended for the vulgar, and not for the cultured classes, to which your Imperial Highness belongs. Even the priests themselves do not believe in the existence of the gods at whose altars they minister; so that Cicero, you will remember, said that ' he wondered how one augur could look in the face of another without laughing.' "

" I quite admit," remarked Adauctus, " that the priests are often impostors, deceiving the people; but our wisest philosophers—the thoughtful Pliny, the profound Tacitus, the sage Seneca, and even the eloquent Cicero whom you have quoted—teach the probability if not the certainty of a future state, where virtue shall be rewarded and wickedness punished."

" What do they know about it any more than any of us ? " interrupted the truculent Naso, to whom ethical themes were by no means familiar or welcome. My creed is embodied in the words of that clever fellow, Juvenal, that I used to learn at school—

' Esse aliquid manes, et subterranea regna,
   Nec pueri credunt, nisi qui nondum ære lavantur.' '*

"What's the use of all this talk ? " lisped a languid-looking epicurean fop, who, sated with dissipation, at twenty-five found life as empty as a sucked orange. " We cannot alter fate. Life is short; let us make the most of it. I'd like to press its nectar into a single draught and have

* *Sat.* ii. 49. " That the manes are anything, or the nether world anything, not even boys believe, unless those still in the nursery."

done with it for ever. As the easy-going Horace says, 'The same thing happens to us all. When our name, sooner or later, has issued from the fatal urn, we leave our woods, our villa, our pleasant homes, and enter the bark which is to bear us into eternal exile !" *

Here the Emperor made an impatient gesture, to indicate that he was weary of this philosophic discourse. At the signal the ladies rose and retired. Adauctus also made his official duties an excuse for leaving the table, where Diocletian and his other guests lingered for hours in a drunken symposium.

Thus we find that the very questions which engage the agnostics and skeptics and pessimists of the present age—the Mallocks, and Cliffords, and Harrisons and their tribe—have agitated the world from the very dawn of philosophy. Did space permit, we might cite the theories of Lucretius as a strange anticipation of the development hypothesis. Indeed the writings of Pyrrho, Porphyry and Celsus show us that the universal tendency of human philosophy, unaided by divine inspiration, is to utter skepticism.

---

* See that saddest but most beautiful of the ode of Horace, To Delius, II. 3 :

> . . . . Et nos in æternum
> Exilium impositura cymbæ.

CHAPTER V.

" THE CHRISTIANS TO THE LIONS."

THE progress of our story transports us, on the day after the banquet described in our last chapter, to the palace of the Prefect Naso, on the Aventine. It was a large and pompous-looking building, with a many-columned portico and spacious gardens, both crowded with statuary, the spoil of foreign cities, or the product of degenerate Greek art—as offensive in design as skilful in execution. The whole bore evidence of the ostentation of vulgar wealth rather than of judicious taste. A crowd of " clients " and satellites of the great man were hanging round the doors, eager to present some petition, proffer some service, or to swell his idle retinue, like jackals around a lion, hoping to pick up a living as hangers-on of such a powerful and unscrupulous dispenser of patronage. In the degenerate

days of the Empire, the civic officials especially
had always a swarm of needy dependents seeking
to batten on the spoils of office. They were
supposed, in some way, to add to the dignity
of the consuls and prætors, as in later times
were the retainers of a mediæval baron. The
system of slavery had made all honest labour
opprobrious, and these idle, corrupt, and dangerous parasites had to be kept in good humour by
lavish doles and constant amusements. "Bread
and the Circus," was their imperious demand,
and having these, they cared for nothing else.

On the morning in question there was con-
siderable excitement among this turbulent throng,
for the rumour was current that there was to
be an examination of certain prisoners accused
of the vile crime of Christianity; and there were
hopes that the criminals would supply fresh
victims for the games of the amphitheatre, which
for some time had languished for lack of suitable
material. The temper of the mob we may learn
by the remarks that reach our ears as we elbow
our way through.

"Ho, Davus! what's the news to-day?" asked
a cobbler with his leathern apron tucked up
about his waist, of a greasy-looking individual
who strutted about with much affectation of
dignity; "you have the run of his Excellency's
kitchen, and ought to know."

"Are *you* there, Samos?" (a nick-name meaning Flat Nose). "Back to your den, you slave, and don't meddle with gentlemen. '*Ne sutor,*' you know the rest."

"Can't you see that the cook drove him out with the basting ladle?" said Muscus, the stout-armed blacksmith, himself a slave, and resenting the insult to his class; and so the laugh was turned against the hungry parasite.

"Here, good Max, you are on the guard, you can tell us," went on the burly smith.

"News enough, as you'll soon find. There's to be more hunting of the Christians for those who like it. For my part, I don't."

"Why not," asked Burdo, the butcher, a truculent looking fellow with a great knife in a sheath at his girdle. "I'd like no better fun. I'd as lief kill a Christian as kill a calf."

"It might suit your business," answered stout Max, with a sneer, "but hunting women and children is not a soldier's trade."

"O ho! that's the game that's a-foot!" chuckled a withered little wretch with a hungry face and cruel eyes, like a weasel. "Here's a chance for an honest man who worships the old gods to turn an honest penny."

"Honest man!" growled Max. "Diogenes would want a good lantern to find one in Rome to-day. He'd certainly never take thee for one.

Thy very face would convict thee of violating all the laws in the Twelve Tables."

"Hunting the Christians, that's the game, is it?" said an ill-dressed idler, blear-eyed and besotted; "and pestilent vermin they are. I'd like to see them all drowned in the Tiber like so many rats."

"You are more likely to see them devoured in the amphitheatre," said Bruto, a Herculean gladiator. "The Prefect is going to give some grand games on the Feast of Neptune. Our new lions will have a chance to flesh their teeth in the bodies of the Christians. The wretches havn't the courage to fight, like the Dacian prisoners, with us gladiators, nor even with the beasts; but just let themselves be devoured like sheep."

At this juncture a commotion was observed about the door, and Naso, the Prefect, came forth and looked haughtily around. Several clients pressed forward with petitions, which he carelessly handed unopened to his secretary, who walked behind. He regarded with some interest the elegantly-dressed and graceful youth who glided through the throng and presented a scroll, saying, as he did so—

"It is of much importance, your Excellency. It is about the Christians."

"Follow me to the Forum," said the Prefect,

and our old acquaintance Isidorus, for it was he, fell into the train of the great civic dignitary. Arrived at the Basilica Julia, or great Court of Justice, the Prefect beckoned to the young Greek secretary, and entered a private ante-room. Throwing himself into a bronze chair, and pointing the Greek to a marble seat, he asked abruptly—

"Now, what is this you know about these Christians ?"

"Something of much importance to your Excellency, and I hope to learn something still more important."

"You shall be well paid if you do," said the Prefect. "It is difficult to convict them of any crime."

"I have secret sources of information, your Excellency. In fact, I hope to bring you the names of the ringleaders of the accursed sect."

"How so? Are you not the secretary of Flaccus Sertorius ?"

"I am, your Excellency, but he has no heart in the work of this new edict. I would like to see more zeal in the Emperor's service."

"I like not this Sertorius," said the Prefect, half musing. "He affects too much what they call the severe old Roman virtues to suit these times. But how do you expect to learn the secrets of these Christians ?"

"By becoming one myself, your Excellency," replied the Greek, with a sinister expression in his eyes.

"By becoming one yourself!" exclaimed the Prefect, in a tone of anger and surprise. Then noting the wily expression of the supple Greek, he added, "Oh! I see, by becoming a spy upon their practices and a betrayer of their secrets. Is that it?"

"We Greeks like not the words traitor and spy," said the youth, with a faint blush, "but to serve the Emperor and your Excellency we would bear even that opprobrium."

"Well, you look capable of it," said the Prefect, with an undisguised sneer, "and I will gladly use any instruments to crush this vile sect."

"But, your Excellency," said the cringing Greek, swallowing his chagrin and annoyance, "I shall require gold to gain the confidence of these Christians—not to bribe them, for that is impossible, but to spend in what they call charity—to give to their sick and poor."

"Not forgetting yourself, I'll be bound," sneered the Prefect. "But what you say is no doubt true;" and turning to the table he wrote an order upon the Imperial Exchequer, and handed it to the Greek, with the words, "If you make good use of that, there is more where it comes from. The Emperor pays his *faithful* servants well." Then dismissing the treacherous tool whom he himself despised, he passed into the Basilica, or court, where the bold Christian youth who had torn down the Emperor's edict was . to receive his sentence.

Livid with the torture he had undergone to make him disclose the names of his accomplices —tortures which he had borne with heroic fortitude—he boldly avowed his act, and defied the power of the Prefect to extort the name of a single Christian from his lips. We will not harrow the hearts of our readers by recounting the atrocious tortures by which the body of the brave youth had been wrung. He was at length borne away fainting to his cruel fate. Although the Prefect, who had sworn to have his secret if he tore the heart out of his body, gnashed his teeth in impotent rage at the defiance of the mangled martyr, yet he could not in his inmost soul help feeling the vast gulf between his sublime fidelity and the heinous guilt of the base traitor from whom he had just parted.

The pages of the contemporary historians, Eusebius and Lactantius, give too minute and circumstantial accounts of the persecutions, of which they were eye-witnesses, to allow us to adopt the complacent theory of Gibbon, that the sufferings of the Christians were compara-

4

tively few and insignificant. "We ou.selves
have seen," says the Bishop of Cæsarea, "crowds
of persons, some beheaded, others burned alive
in a single day, so that the murderous weapons
were blunted and broken to pieces, and the executioners, weary with slaughter, were obliged to
give over the work of blood. . . . They vied
with each other," he continues, "in inventing
new tortures, as if there were prizes offered to
him who should contrive the greatest cruelties."*
Men whose only crime was their religion, were
scourged with chains laden with bronze balls,
till the flesh hung in shreds, and even the bones
were broken. They were bound in fetters of
red hot iron, and roasted over fires so slow
that they lingered for hours, or even days, in
their mortal agony; their flesh was scraped from
the very bone with ragged shells, or lacerated
with burning pincers, iron hooks, and instruments
with horrid teeth and claws, hence called *ungulæ*,
examples of which have been found in the Catacombs; molten metal was applied to their bodies
till they became one undistinguishable wound,
and mingled salt and vinegar,† or unslacked
lime, were rubbed upon the quivering flesh, torn

---

* Euseb. Hist. Eccles., viii. 7.
† "Salt me the more, that I may be incorruptible,"
said Tarachus, the martyr, as he underwent this excruciating torture.

and bleeding from the rack or scourge—tortures
more inhuman than savage Indian ever wreaked
upon his mortal foe.　Chaste matrons and tender
virgins were given over to a fate a thousand-fold
worse than death, and were subjected to indignities too horrible for words to utter.　And all
these sufferings were endured, often with joy and
exultation, for the love of a Divine Master, when
a single word, a grain of incense cast upon the
heathen altar, would have released the victims
from their agonies.　No lapse of time, and no
recoil from the idolatrous homage paid in after
ages to the martyr's relics, should impair in
our hearts the profound and rational reverence
with which we bend before his tomb.

While the examination of the Christian martyr
was in progress, much interest was manifested
in his fate by the throng of idlers who were
wont to linger around the public courts, to gratify
their curiosity or their morbid love of cruelty.

"The State is in danger," said Piso, the barber,
gesticulating violently, "if such miscreants are
suffered to live."

"Ay, is it," chimed in a garrulous pedagogue,
"this is rank treason."

"Right, neighbour Probus," added a petti-
fogging lawyer.　"This is the very *crimen
majestatis*.　These men are the enemies of Cæsar
and of the Roman people."

"Who would think he was so wicked?" said a poor freed-woman who sold sugar barley in the Forum. "Sure he looks innocent enough."

"He *is* innocent," replied her neighbour, who kept a stall for the sale of figs and olives. "'Tis that wretch who is wicked," looking fiercely at the Prefect as he moved from the court.

"You are right," said a grave-looking man, speaking low, but with a look of secret understanding; "but be careful. You can do the brave Lucius no good, and may betray the others into jeopardy," and he passed swiftly through the throng.

"'Tis time all these Atheists were exterminated," said Furbo, a sort of hanger-on at the neighbouring temple of Saturn. "The gods are angry, and the victims give sinister auspices. To-day when the priest slew the ram for the sacrifice, would you believe it? it had no heart; and the sacred chickens refused their food."

"And they certainly are to blame for the floods of the Tiber, which destroyed all the olives and lentils in my shop," said Fronto, the oil and vegetable seller.

"And the rain rusted all the wheat on our farm," said Macer, the villicus or land-steward.

"And the fever has broken out afresh in the Suburra," croaked a withered old Egyptian crone, like a living mummy, who told fortunes and sold spells in that crowded and pest-smitten quarter, where the poor swarmed like flies.

"And the drought has blighted all the vines," echoed Demetrius, the wine-merchant.

"I never knew trade so dull," whined Ephraim, the Jewish money-lender. "We'll never have good times again till these accursed Christians are all destroyed."

"So say I," "And I," "And I," shouted one after another of the mob, till the wild cry rang round the Forum, "*Christiani adleones*"—"The Christians to the lions."*

* "If the Tiber overflows its banks," says Tertullian, "or if the Nile does not; if there be drought or earthquakes, famine or pestilence, the cry is raised, 'the Christians to the lions.' But I pray you," he adds, in refutation of these absurd charges, "were misfortunes unknown before Tiberius? The true God was not worshipped when Hannibal conquered at Cannæ, or the Gauls filled the city."—Tertul. *Apol.*, x.

CHAPTER VI.

THE MARTYR'S BURIAL.

THE fawning Greek Isidorus had stealthily wormed his way into the confidence of Faustus, a servant of Adauctus, by professing to be, if not a Christian, at least a sincere inquirer after the truth, and an ardent hater of the edict of persecution. Faustus had therefore promised to conduct him to a private meeting of the Christians, where he might be more fully instructed by the good presbyter, Primitius. In the short summer twilight they therefore made their way to the villa of the Christian matron Marcella, on the Appian Way, about two miles from the city gates. A high wall surrounded the grounds. In this was a wicket or door, at which Faustus knocked. The white-haired porter partly opened the door, and recognizing the foremost figure, admitted him, but gave a look of inquiry before passing his companion.

"It is all right," said Faustus. "He is a good friend of mine," and so they passed on.

The grounds were large and elegant, fountains flashed in the soft moonlight, the night-blooming cereus breathed forth its rare perfume, and masses of cypress and ilex cast deep shadows on the pleached alleys. But there was a conspicuous absence of the garden statuary invariably found in pagan grounds. There was no figure of the god Terminus, nor of the beautiful Flora, or Pomona, nor of any of the fair goddesses which to-day people the galleries of Rome. In the spacious *atrium,* or central apartment of the house, which was partially lighted by bronze candalabra, was gathered a company of nearly a hundred persons, seated on couches around the hall—the men on the right and the women on the left. A solemn stillness brooded over 'the entire assembly. Near a tall cadalabrum stood a venerable figure with a snowy beard —the presbyter Primitius. From a parchment scroll in his hand he read in impressive tones the holy words of hope and consolation, "Let not your hearts be troubled, ye believe in God, believe also in me," and the rest of that sweet, parting counsel of the world's Redeemer.

Before he was through, a procession with

torches was seen approaching through the garden.
On a bier, borne by four young men, lay the
body of Lucius the martyr, wrapped in white

STAIRWAY TO CATACOMB.

and strewn with flowers—at rest in the solemn
majesty of death from the tortures of the rack
and scourge. The little assembly within joined

the procession without, and softly singing the
holy words which still give such consolation
to the stricken heart, "Beati sunt mortui qui
in Domino morientur—Blessed are the dead who
die in the Lord," through the shadowy cypress
alleys wound the solemn procession. Soon it
reached an archway, like that shown in our first
chapter, the entrance to the catacomb of St.
Callixtus, which lay beneath the grounds of the
Lady Marcella. Then, preceded by torches, with
careful tread the bearers of the bier slowly descended a rock-hewn stairway, and traversed a
long and gloomy corridor, lined on either side
with the graves of the dead.* This stairway
and corridor are shown in the engravings which
accompany this chapter.

An almost supernatural fear fell upon the soul
of Isidorus the Greek, who had followed in the
train of the procession, as it penetrated further
and further into the very heart of the earth.
He seemed like Ulysses with his ghostly guide
visiting the grim regions of the nether-world,
and the words of the classic poet came to his
mind, " Horror on all sides, the very silence fills
the soul with dread." Already for more than
two centuries these gloomy galleries had been
the receptacles of the Christian dead, and in

* For the details above given, see Bingham's *Origines
Ecclesiastica.*

many places the slabs that sealed the tombs were broken, and the graves yawned weirdly as he passed, revealing the unfleshed skeletons lying on their stony bed. To his excited imagination they seemed to menace him with their outstretched bony arms. Deep, mysterious shadows crouched around, full of vague suggestions of affright. His gay, joyous and pleasure-loving nature recoiled from the evidences of mortality around him. His footsteps faltered, and he almost fell to the rocky pavement. The procession swept on, the glimmering lights growing dimmer and dimmer, and then turning an angle they suddenly disappeared. Fear lent wings to his feet, and he fled along the narrow path with outstretched hands, sometimes touching with a feeling of horrible recoil the bones or ashes of the dead. He hurried along, groping from side to side, and when he reached the passage down which the funeral procession had disappeared, no gleam of it was visible, nor could he tell, so suddenly the lights had disappeared, whether it had turned to the right or to the left. The darkness was intense—a darkness that might be felt, a brooding horror that oppressed every sense. He tried to call out, but his tongue seemed to cleave to the roof of his mouth, and his faint cry was swallowed up in the deep and oppressive silence. Had the vengeance of the

gods overtaken him in punishment for his me-
ditated crime?   Was he, who so loved the light
and air, and joyous sunshine, never to behold

CORRIDOR OF CATACOMB.

them again?   Must he be buried in these gloomy
vaults for ever?   These thoughts surged through
his brain, and almost drove him wild.   But
what sounds are those that steal faintly on his

ear? They seem like the music of heaven heard
in the heart of hell. Stronger, sweeter, clearer,
come the holy voices. And now they shape
themselves to words, "Nam et si ambulavero in
medio umbræ mortis, non timebo mala—Yea,
though I walk through the valley of the shadow
of death, I will fear no evil." Was it to taunt
his terrors those strange words were sung? Then
the holy chant went on, "Quonian tu, mecum es.
Virga tua, et baculus tuus, ipsa me consolata
sunt—For thou art with me, thy rod and thy
staff they comfort me." What strange secret had
these Christians that sustained their souls even
surrounded by the horrors of the tomb?

Isidorus groped his way amid the gloom toward
these heavenly sounds. Soon he caught a faint
glimmer of light reflected from an angle of the
corridor, and then a ray through an open doorway
pierced the gloom. Hurrying forward he found
the whole company from which he had become
separated gathered in a sort of chapel hewn out
of the solid rock. The body of Lucius lay upon
the bier before an open tomb, hewn out of the
wall. The venerable presbyter, by the fitful
torchlight which illumined the strange group, and
lit up the pious paintings and epitaphs upon the
wall, read from a scroll the strange words, "And
I saw under the altar the souls of them that
were slain for the Word of God and for the

testimony which they held, and they cried with a loud voice, saying, How long, O Lord, holy and true, dost thou not judge and avenge our blood on them that dwell on the earth ?" A great fear fell upon the soul of the susceptible Greek, for the slain man seemed, in the solemn majesty of death, to become an accusing judge.

Then turning his scroll the presbyter read on, "What are these arrayed in white robes and whence came they ? These are they which came out of great tribulation, and have washed their robes and made them white in the blood of the Lamb. Therefore are they before the throne of God, and serve Him day and night in His temple. . . They shall hunger no more, neither thirst any more, . . and God shall wipe away all tears from their eyes."

These holy words stirred strange emotions in the agitated breast of the young Greek. Sweeter were they than ought he had ever read in Pindar's page, and more sublime than even Homer's hymns. If these things were true, he thought, he would gladly change places with the martyr on his bier, if only he might exchange the torturing ambitions, strifes and sins of time for the holy joys which that marvellous scroll revealed.

Then by loving hands the martyr's body was placed in its narrow tomb. A marble slab, on which were simply written his name and the words, "DORMIT IN PACE—He sleeps in peace," was cemented against the opening. With a trowel, a palm branch, the symbol of martyrdom, was rudely traced in the yet unhardened cement, and the little company began to disperse.

"O sir," cried the young Greek, clasping the hand of the venerable Primitius, "teach me more fully this excellent way."

"Gladly, my son," replied the benignant old man. "Come hither to-morrow. For here," he added with a smile, "my friends insist that I must remain concealed till this outburst of. persecution shall have passed.* Hilarus, the fossor, will be thy guide. He will now conduct thee back to thy friend Faustus, who is seeking thee."

By the dim light of a waxen taper which he carried, Hilarus led the Greek to the entrance to the Catacomb, where they found Faustus waiting in some alarm at the delay of his friend. In the bright moonlight they walked back to the city. Isidorus thought well to evade giving an account of his adventure in the Catacomb, and, to turn the conversation, asked how the Christians had obtained the body of Lucius from the public executioner.

* Liberius, Bishop of Rome, lay concealed in the Catacombs for a whole year, during a time of persecution.

"Oh, money will do anything in Rome," said Faustus, at which the Greek visibly winced. "The Lady Marcella, in whose grounds the Catacomb is, devotes much of her wealth to burying the poor of the Church, and her steward had no difficulty in purchasing from Hanno, the executioner, the mangled remains of the martyr. 'Tis like, before long, that he will have many such to sell."

CHAPTER VII.

WITH HILARUS THE FOSSOR.

"NO one becomes vile all at once," said the Roman moralist, and we would be unjust to the fickle, fawning Greek Isidorus, if we concluded that deliberate treachery was his purpose, as, at the invitation of Primitius, he repaired next day to the catacomb of St. Calixtus. His was a susceptible, impressionable nature, easily influenced by its environment, like certain substances that acquire the odour, fragrant or foul, of the atmosphere by which they are surrounded. Amid the vileness of the Roman court, his better feelings died, and he was willing to become the minion of tyranny, or the tool of treachery. Amid the holy influences of the Christian assembly, some chord responded, like an Eolian harp, to the breathings of the airs from heaven. It was, therefore, with strangely conflicting feelings, that he passed beneath the Capuan Gate, and along the Appian

Way, toward the Villa Marcella. His better nature recoiled from his purposed treachery of the previous day. His heart yearned to know more of that strange power which sustained the Christian martyr in the presence of torture and of death.

He was recognized by the porter at the gate of the villa as the companion of Faustus, and on his inquiry for the house of Hilarus, the fossor, was directed to a low-walled, tile-roofed building, such as may be seen in many parts of the Campagna to the present day. About the house were many stone chippings, and numerous slabs of marble. Under a sort of arbour, covered with vine branches in full leaf, stood a grisly-visaged man, with close-cropped, iron-gray hair, chipping with mallet and chisel at a large sarcophagus, or stone coffin, upon a mason's bench.

"Do I address Hilarus, the fossor?" asked the Greek, with a graceful salutation.

"I am Hilarus, at your service, noble sir," replied the old man, with a kindly expression of countenance.

The young Greek then told of the invitation given him by the good presbyter, Primitius, and requested to be conducted to him.

"You are, of course, known to the porter, or you would not have obtained admission to these grounds," said Hilarus. "But you will first honour my poor roof by partaking some refreshment after your hot walk from the city."

"Thanks, good friend," replied the Greek, "a draught of your native wine would not be amiss. Nay, I would prefer it here beneath the grateful shadow of this vine," he continued, as Hilarus courteously led the way to the open door of the cottage. This was quite small, and had almost no furniture save some earthen pots for cooking at an open fireplace. In a moment the old man re-appeared with an earthen flagon of wine and a bronze salver, with bread and goat's milk cheese, and a bronze cup.*

"For whom is this elegant sarcophagus?" asked Isidorus, as he sipped his wine.

"I pray it be not for her who orders it," said the old man, devoutly; "at least not for many a long day to come. The good Lady Marcella bade me exercise my best skill in setting forth the great truths of the Gospel, that in death as in life, she said, she might teach the doctrines of Christ. She often comes to see how I get on with it, and to describe how she wishes it to be.

---

* Just such a peasant's house the writer visited on the Appian Way, near this spot, and just such a repast he shared at the entrance of this very catacomb. "The wine," said the guide, "is necessary to guard against a chill." The contrast between the temperature above ground and below was about 30°.

SARCOPHAGUS NOW IN LATERAN MUSEUM.

See," said the old man, pointing to the side— (see cut in margin,)— "the general idea is all her own, the details only are mine. These four groups exhibit four scenes in the life — or rather in the death — of our Lord. To the extreme right we see Pilate, warned by his wife, washing his hands and saying 'I am innocent of the blood of this just person,' and yet, like a coward, consenting to His death, he was as guilty as Judas, who betrayed Him."

At this the Greek visibly winced, then paled and flushed, and said, "Well, what is the next group?"

"That is part of the same," said the sculptor, with evident pride in his work. "It represents our Lord, guarded by a Roman soldier, witnessing a good confession before Pontius Pilate. In the central niche are two soldiers, types of the Chris-

tian warriors, whose only place of safety is beneath
the cross; while above are the wreath of victory,
the doves of peace, and the sacred monogram,
made up, I need not tell you, who are a Greek,
of the two first letters of the word Christos. To
the left you observe a Roman soldier, putting on
Jesus the crown of thorns, and in the last, Simon
the Cyrenian, guarded by a soldier, bearing His
cross." *

"And for whom are all these funeral tablets,"
said Isidorus, pointing to a number of slabs partly
executed—some with the engraved outline of a
dove, or fish, or anchor, or olive branch upon
them—leaning against the wall.

"For whom God pleases," said the old man,
devoutly. "I keep them ready to suit purchasers,
and then I have only to fill the name and age, or
date."

"But see here," said the Greek, touching with
his foot one on which were effigies of Castor and
Pollux, the "great twin brethren" of the Roman
mythology, and the letters, "DIS MANIBVS—To
the Divine Spirits;" "this is a pagan inscription.
How come you to use that?"

"Oh, we turn up such slabs by scores, in

* This sarcophagus, with many others resembling it
the writer studied minutely in the Lateran Museum at
Rome.

ploughing the fields hereabout. They may be hundreds of years old, for aught I know. We just turn that side to the wall, or deface it with a few strokes of the chisel."

"It was a prentice hand that made *that*, I'll be bound," said the Greek, pointing to one on which was rudely painted in black pigment, the sprawling inscription that follows, no two letters being the same size—

LOcvSAVGvSTIsvToRis.

"The Place of Augustus, the Shoemaker."

"Oh, that is the epitaph of a poor cobbler. I ιet my boys do that for nothing. They will soon be able to do better. Here now is one by my oldest son, of which I would not be ashamed myself;" and he pointed to a neatly-cut inscription, the letters coloured with a bright vermillion pigment, which ran thus,—

AVRELIAE THEVDOSIAE

BENIGNISSIMAE ET INCOMPARABILI FEMINAE

AVRELIVS OPTATVS

CONIVGE INNOCENTISSIMAE

"Aurelius Optatus, to his most innocent wife, Aurelia Theudosia, a most gracious and incomparable woman."

"We will now, if you are sufficiently cool," he went on, "enter the catacomb. It is not well to make too sudden a transition from this sultry heat to their chilly depths."

"Thanks," said the young man, "I shall find the change from this sultry air, I doubt not, very agreeable;" and they crossed a vineyard under a blazing sun, that made the cool crypts exceedingly grateful. Descending the stairway, the guide took from a niche a small terra-cotta lamp, which he carefully trimmed and lit at another, which was always kept burning there.*

"Is there not danger of losing one's way in this labyrinth?" asked the Greek, feeling no small degree of the terror of his late adventure returning.

"Very great danger, indeed," replied Hilarus, "unless you know the clue and marks by which we steer, almost like ships at sea. But knowing these, the way may become as familiar as the streets of Rome. You may, perhaps, have heard of Cæcilia, a blind girl, who acted as guide to these subterranean places of assembly, because to her accustomed feet the path was as easy as the Appian Way to those who see."

* The writer has some of these earthen lamps which once did service in the Catacombs. They bear Christian symbols, inscribed before baking—a dove, anchor, olive branch, fish, and the like.

"How many Greek epitaphs there are," said
Isidorus, deeply interested in scanning the inscriptions as he passed.

"Yes," said the fossor, "there are a-many of
your countryfolk buried here; and even some
who are not like to have their epitaphs written
in the language in which holy Paulus wrote his
epistle to the Church in Rome."

"But what wretched scrawls the most of them
are," said the Greek, with something like a sneer;
"and see, here is one even upside down."

"Yes, noble sir," continued the old man, "not
many mighty, not many noble are called—most
of those who sleep around us are God's great
family of the poor. Indeed, most of them were
slaves. That poor fellow was a martyr in the
last persecution. I mind it well, though it is
years agone. We buried him by stealth at dead
of night, and did not notice that the hastily
written inscription was reversed."

The dim rays of their lamp and taper made
but a faint ring of light about their feet. Their
steps, as they walked over the rocky floor, echoed
strangely down the long-drawn corridors and hollow vaults, dying gradually away in the solemn
stillness of this valley of the shadow of death.
The sudden transition from the brilliant Italian
sunlight to this sepulchral gloom, from the busy
city of the living to this silent city of the dead,

smote the heart of the susceptible youth with a feeling of awe. And all around in this vast necropolis, each in his narrow cell forever laid, were

SECTIONAL VIEW OF GALLERY AND CHAMBERS, SHOWING LIGHT AND AIR SHAFT.

unnumbered thousands, who were once like himself, full of energy and life.

As they advanced, a faint light in the distance seemed to penetrate the gloom. It grew brighter

as they approached, and attracted by the sound
of the footsteps, a venerable figure emerged from
a doorway and stood in the flood of light which
poured down from an opening in the vaulted
roof, which extended to the bright free air above.
Almost like an apparition from the other world,
in the strong, Rembrandt-like illumination in
which he stood, looked the venerable Primitius,
clothed in white, with silvery hair and flowing
beard, and high, bare brow. As Isidorus glanced
up the shaft, he saw the blue sky shining far
above, and the waving of the long grass that
fringed the opening for light and air. This construction—a very frequent one in the Catacombs—
is shown in sectional view on the previous page.
On each side of the corridor was a chamber about
twelve feet square, also lit up by this shaft,
which, plastered with white stucco, reflected the
light into every part.

"Welcome, my son," said the venerable presbyter, as he sat down on a bench hewn out of
the dry pummice-like rock. "Welcome to these
abodes of death; may they prove to thee the
birthplace to eternal life;" and he laid his hand
benignantly on the head of the young man; whom
he had motioned to a seat beside him.

"Sire," said the youth, all the nobler feelings
of his nature deeply moved, "I wish above all
things to sit at your feet and to learn the lessons

of wisdom which you are so well able to impart. But are these seemly surroundings for a man of your years and condition ?—this rocky vault, this utter loneliness, and these crumbling relics of mortality ?" and he shuddered as he glanced at the shattered sepulchral slabs, which revealed the remains of what was once man in his strength, woman in her beauty, or a sweet child in its innocence and glee.

"Why not, my son ? soon I must lie down with them and be at rest. The thought has no terrors to my soul. I know no loneliness, and through the care of kind friends my wants are all supplied. But your young blood and sensitive imagination, I perceive, shrink from these things to which, by long use, I have become accustomed. Let us go into the adjoining chamber, which you will find more cheerful, and, I trust, not less instructive."

CEILING PAINTING FROM CATACOMB OF ST. CALIXTUS, ROME.

CHAPTER VIII.

WITH PRIMITIUS, THE PRESBYTER.

THE venerable presbyter laid his hand familiarly on the young man's shoulder and conducted him into a smaller, but much more elegantly finished, apartment. It contained no graves, save an arched tomb which had never been used ; at one side was a shelf for lamps. The whole surface of the wall was covered with hard white stucco, which was divided into panels by bands and borders of brilliant red and blue, as shown in the cut on next page. The vaulted ceiling was similarly divided. The angles were filled in with elegant floral designs, and the panels with Biblical and symbolical paintings, which Primitius began now to explain.

"Thou seest, my son," he said, " that central group above the arch. That represents the Good Shepherd who gave His life for the sheep. Thou perceivest He bears the lost sheep upon His shoulders, and gently leads those which follow Him. Even so, all we, like sheep, have gone astray, but the blessed Saviour seeks the erring, and brings them into the safe and true fold.

PAINTED CHAMBER IN THE CATACOMBS.

Thou seest to the left the figure between the two lions. That is Daniel in the lion's den; and to the right are the three Hebrews in the fiery furnace. These, my son, are symbols of the

Church of Christ, amid the wild beasts and the
fires of persecutions. But she shall be delivered
unhurt; she shall come forth unscathed. In the
ceiling you will observe praying figures between
lambs, the emblems of the Church, the Bride
which is the Lamb's wife, perpetually engaged
in adoration and prayer."

The youth was deeply impressed, and almost
awed, to see the silvery-haired old man, a refugee
from persecution, in these subterranean crypts,
with the full assurance of faith, confronting all
the power of the persecuting despot of the world,
and predicting the triumph of that oppressed
Church which was compelled to seek safety in
those dens and caves of the earth.

The good old man then sought to impart the
great truths of our holy religion to his new
catechumen, and to implant in his soul the same
germs of lofty faith that flourished in his own.
With this object he led him through the long
corridors and chambers of the vast encampment
of death—a sort of whispering gallery of the
past, eloquent with the expression of the faith
and hope of the silent sleepers in their narrow
cells.

"Listen, my son," said Primitius, "to the testimony of the dead in Christ, and of the martyrs
for the truth," and pausing from time to time
before some inscribed or painted slab, he pointed

out the lofty hopes which sustained their souls
in the very presence of death.

"Here," he said, entering again the chamber
he had first left, "is the sepulchre of my own
beloved wife. When depressed and lonely, I
come hither and derive strength and consolation
by reading the words which she requested, with
her dying breath, should be written on her tomb,"
and with deep emotion he traced with his finger
the inscription :—*

PARCITE VOS LACRIMIS DVLCIS CVM CONIVGE NATAE
VIVENTEMQVE DEO CREDITE FLERE NEFAS.

"Refrain from tears, my sweet children and husband,
and believe that it is forbidden to weep for one who lives
in God."

"And here," he went on, "is the tomb of our
little child," and Isidorus read with softened
spirit the words :—

AGNELLVS DEI—PARVM STETIT APVD NOS ET
PRAECESSIT NOS IN PACE.

"God's little lamb—he stayed but a short time with
us, and went before us in peace."

"And here," said Primitius, "is the couch of

---

* The following, except the last one, are all authentic
inscriptions from the Catacombs, selected from many
hundreds, translated by the writer in his volume on this
subject.

our eldest daughter," and he read, with caressing tones, her epitaph :—

ANIMA DVLCIS INNOCVA SAPIENS ET PVLCHRA—
NON MORTVA SED DATA SOMNO.

"A sweet spirit, guileless, wise, beautiful She is not dead but sleepeth."

" This is certainly very different," said Isidorus, "from two epitaphs I read to-day upon the pagan tombs on the Appian Way.   They ran thus :—

DECIPIMVR VOTIS ET TEMPORE FALLIMVR ET MORS
DERIDET CVRAS ANXIA VITA NIHIL.

" We are deceived by our vows, misled by time, and death derides our cares ; anxious life is naught."

INFANTI DVLCISSIMO QVEM DEI IRATI AETERNO
SOMNO DEDERVNT.

" To a very sweet child, whom the angry gods gave to eternal sleep."

" Yes," said Primitius, "nothing can sustain the soul in the presence of death, but such faith as that of my friend Eutuchius, who sleeps here ;" and he read the lofty line :—

IN CHRISTVM CREDENS PREMIA LVCIS HABET.

" Believing in Christ, he has the rewards of the light (of heaven)."

" Similar are these also," and he pointed to the following ill-written, but sublime, epitaphs, which Isidorus slowly spelled out :—

DVLCIS ET INNOCES (*sic*) HIC DORMIT SEVERIANVS
SOMNO PACIS CVIVS SPIRITVS IN LVCE DOMINI
SVSCEPTVS EST,—IN SEMPETERNALE
AEVVM QVIESCIT SECVRVS.

"Here lies in the sleep of peace, the sweet and
innocent Severianus, whose spirit is received into the
light of God. He rests free from care throughout endless time."

"But how were these Christians so confident
of the future life," asked the Greek, "when the
greatest of the philosophers and sages—a Socrates
or Cicero—never rose above a vague 'perhaps,'
and even the philosophic Pliny, anticipating only
annihilation, writes, 'there is no more conscious-
ness after death than before birth?'"

"Find there thy answer, young man," exclaimed
Primitius, and with a gleam of exultation in his
eyes, he pointed to the following epitaphs:—

CREDO QVIA REDEMPTOR MEVS VIVIT ET NOVISSIMO
DIE DE TERRA SVSCITABIT ME IN CARNE MEA
VIDEBO DOMINVM.

"I believe, because that my Redeemer liveth, and in
the last day shall raise me from the earth, that in my
flesh I shall see the Lord."

HIC REQVIESCIT CARO MEA NOVISSIMO VERO DIE
PER CHRISTVM CREDO RECVSCITABITVR A MORTVIS.

"Here rests my flesh, but at the last day, through
Christ, I believe it will be raised from the dead."

"And must the soul, then, slumber with the body in blank unconsciousness till this 'last day?'" asked the Greek.   "Methinks I should shudder at going out into the dark inane, like a taper extinguished in these gloomy vaults. Better is the dim and ghostly Hades, and Elysian Fields of our own mythology, than that."

"Not so, my son," replied Primitius, "we believe with the blessed Paul—that as soon as the soul passes from earth's living death, it enters into the undying life and unfading bliss of heaven." And he pointed out, one after another, the following epitaphs corroborating his view :—

CORPVS HABET TELLVS ANIMAM CAELESTIA REGNA
MENS NESCIA MORTIS VIVIT ET ASPECTV
FRVITVR BENE CONSCIA CHRISTI.

"The soul lives unknowing of death, and consciously rejoices in the vision of Christ."

PRIMA VIVIS IN GLORIA DEI ET IN PACE DOMINI
NOSTRI XR.

"Prima, thou livest in the glory of God, and in the peace of Christ our Lord."

"This is indeed a high philosophy, beyond aught I ever heard before," said Isidorus, deeply moved.   "Whence do you Christians derive such lofty teachings ? For as Hilarus but now said, most of your sect are poor and lowly in this world's goods and rank."

"Our teaching comes, my son, from God Himself, the Great Father of lights, and from Jesus
Christ our Lord. Behold, as the greatest favour
I can do thee, I will lend thee this precious MS.
of the Gospel of the blessed John;" and he took
from a leathern case a purple vellum parchment
scroll, inscribed with letters of silver. "Cherish
it carefully; 'tis worth more than gold. When
thou hast well pondered it, I will lend thee the
letter of the blessed Paul to the infant Church
in this city of Rome. But here comes Hilarus
to conduct thee back to the light of day. Return
hither, if thou canst, on the fourth day from now
—the day of our Sabbath assembly. My blessing
be upon thee. *Pax vobiscum et cum spiritu tuo.*"

The young Greek knelt at the old man's feet,
then rose and kissed his hand, and followed in
silence the fossor Hilarus. At length he broke
the silence by inquiring,—

"What's the meaning, good Hilarus, of all
these strange figures which I have noted on the
tombstones as I passed. I have observed a lion,
a pig, an ass, a cobbler's last, carpenters', masons',
and wool-combers' implements; a fish, a ship, an
anchor, and the like—all scratched or painted on
the stone slabs. They have no religious signifi-
cance, surely?"

"Well, no, not all of them," said Hilarus, with
a smile. "You see, many of the Christians being

lowly craftsmen, are unable to read, so the tools or emblems of their calling are inscribed on the tombs of their friends, that they may recognize and find them again in this vast cemetery."

" But the ship, anchor, and fish are not signs of a handicraft, unless that of sailor or fisherman."

"No, the fish has another and a secret meaning. I need not tell a scholar like you, that the first letters of the Greek names for Jesus Christ, Son of God, the Saviour, make up the word Ichthus, or fish, so it is used as a secret symbol of our faith. The ship is the emblem, I have been told, even in your own country, of a well-spent life, and to us it signifies a soul entering into the haven of eternal rest. While our holy hopes are the anchor of the soul, both sure and steadfast, entering into that within the veil."

" Well, and the lion, ass, and pig? What about them ?"

" These," said the fossor, with a laugh, which seemed as incongruous to him as it would be to a modern sexton, for such his office virtually was, "these are a sort of play upon the names of Leo, Onager, and Porcella, the latter was a sort of pet name, I suspect—'Little Pig'—by which their friends, who could not read, could find their tombs."

" What wives these Christians must have had," continued the keenly-observing Greek. " I have noticed several inscriptions, in which they are said to have passed ten, twenty, thirty, and one even fifty years of married life—SINE IVRGIO, SINE AEMVLATIONE, SINE DISSIDIO, SINE QVERELA— ' Without contention, without emulation, without dissension, without strife.' There are no such wives in Rome now, I'll be bound—at least in the Rome I am acquainted with."

"Yes," said the old man, with a sigh, " come with me into yonder chapel. I always, in passing this way, stop there to see again the sepulchre of the best wife God ever gave to any man." After walking in silence some minutes, he entered a sort of family vault, and lit a bronze lamp, shaped like a ship, hanging from the vaulted ceiling, while Isidorus studied out the following inscription, not altogether free from errors in spelling and grammar:—

CONIVGE VENEVANDE BONE INNOCVA FLORENTIA
DIGNA PIA AMABILIS PVDICA (*sic*) DEO FIDELIS
DVLCIS MARITO NVTRIX FAMILIAE HVMILIS
CVNCTIS AMATRIX PAVPERVM. BIXIT MECVM
ANN. XXXII. MENS. IX. DIES V. HOR. X.
SCRVPVLOS XII. SEMPER CONCORDES SINE VLLA
QVERELA. BIXIT PLVS MINVS ANN. LII. MENS.
V. INCOMPARABILEM CONIVGEM MALE FRACTVS
CONIVX GEMITV TRISTI LACRI MIS DEFLET.

"To my wife Florentia, deserving of honour, good,

guileless, worthy, pious, amiable, modest, faithful to
God, endeared to her husband, the nurse of her family,
humble to all, a lover of the poor. She lived with me
(*i.e.*, was married) thirty-two years, nine months, five
days, ten hours, six scruples (about a quarter of an hour
—they were very scrupulous about this). She lived
(altogether) fifty-two years, five months, more or less.
The sore-broken husband bewails, with tears and bitter
lamentation, his incomparable spouse."

"Yes, I made it all up, and carved it all
myself," said the old man, as Isidorus finished
reading the long inscription; "and if I say it
myself, I don't think there is a better in the
whole Catacomb; you see, I selected the best
bits from all the best epitaphs, and she deserved
it every word, dear soul," and he drew his rough
hand across his moistened eyes.

The easy-tempered Greek was too good-natured
to inflict wanton pain, so he ignored its bad
Latinity, and contented himself with saying that
"it was indeed a very remarkable epitaph."

In a few minutes they emerged from the gloom
of the Catacomb to the golden glory which was
flooding the broad Campagna from the westering
sun. "Would," thought Isidorus within himself,
"that I could thus emerge from the gloomy
doubts and fears in which my spirit gropes, to
the golden light of Christian life."

CHAPTER IX.

A DIFFICULT QUEST.

THE Empress Valeria had not forgotten her purpose to discover, if possible, the father of her freed-woman, Callirhoë, and at the earliest opportunity took steps to accomplish her design. It was, she knew, a task of much difficulty, and one that required an intelligent and confidential agent. It was also of the utmost importance that some sign of identity should be exhibited as a guarantee of the good faith of the agent. With this view the Empress one day, as she sat at her toilet in the apartment described in our third chapter, thus interrogated her freed-woman and namesake, Valeria Callirhoë.

"Hast thou any token, child," she asked, " by which, should we find thy father, he would be assured of thy identity ? "

" I was despoiled of everything, your Majesty," said the girl, " by the pirates by whom we were captured, except the clothes in which I stood. All my rings and jewellery were rudely snatched away, and I never saw them again."

"What is that little amulet I have seen thee wear?" asked the Empress; "I think thou hast it now."

"Oh, that was so trivial and valueless," said Callirhoë, "that they either overlooked it or thought it not worth taking;" and she drew from the folds of her robe, where it hung suspended by a silken cord about her neck, a cornelian stone, carved into the shape of a tiny fish,* on which was inscribed the word, ΣΩΤΗΡ, or "Saviour," and on the other side the letters, ΚΑΛ.ΔΗΜΗΤ.ΘΥΓ—a contraction for "Callirhoë, daughter of Demetrius."

"Trivial as it is," said the girl, with emotion, "it is something which I value above all price. My sainted mother, before she died, took it from her neck and put it upon mine; and I hope to wear it while I live."

"You do not regard it as an amulet, or charm

---

* These objects, of which the writer has examined several, were given to neophytes on the occasion of their baptism, as an emblem of their holy faith. (See explanation of the symbol of the fish in last chapter, p. 82.) They were often used as a sign of membership in the Christian Church, somewhat like our modern class-tickets.

against evil spirits, I am sure, like some Christians, who have not quite shaken off their pagan superstitions."

"Nay, your Majesty, but as a symbol of our holy faith. Yet it might well be a spell to keep my soul from sin, so sacred are its associations."

"I want you to give it to me," said the Empress.

"It is yours, your Majesty," said the girl, taking it from her neck, and passionately kissing it. "To no one else on earth would I give it; but from my best benefactress I can withhold nothing."

"I would not put thee to the pain of parting with it," said the Empress, with a kind caress, "but I need it as a clue, to find, if possible, thy father, and when found, as an identification of his child. I do not wish to raise hopes which may be doomed to disappointment; but I am about to make a strenuous effort to discover thy sire."

"A thousand thanks, dearest lady," exclaimed the grateful girl, kissing her mistress's hands and bedewing them with her tears. "I feel sure that God will reward your efforts, and answer my ceaseless prayers."

In pursuance of her purpose, the Empress wrote upon a scroll of parchment the following letter to her faithful counsellor, Adauctus :—

"Valeria, consort of the co-Emperor Galerius

Cæsar—to Adauctus, Treasurer of the Imperial Exchequer, greeting:

"Honoured Servant,—Thy mistress hath need of a faithful and intelligent agent, to execute a delicate and difficult mission. He must be of good address, and must be a man whom I can implicitly trust. When thou hast found such, bring him with thee to the palace."

L. S.

Having bound the scroll with a silken cord, and affixed her signet in purple wax, and addressed the document to the Imperial Treasurer, she sent it by a soldier of the guard, whom we would describe in modern parlance as an orderly-in-waiting, to Adauctus.

During the latter part of the day, the chamberlain announced a visit from "His Excellency the Imperial Treasurer." That officer was received with much honour by the Empress, who was attended only by her faithful freedwoman.

"Many thanks, your Excellency, for your prompt attendance. Have you found me the paragon whom I require?"

"I cannot avouch for that, your Majesty, but he is highly commended by his master, an honest soldier, who places him at your Majesty's service. Of his nimble wit and subtle parts, I can myself bear witness, and my own servant testifies that, if not a Christian, he is at least a sincere inquirer after the truth."

The Empress briefly explained the nature of the commission which she wished executed, and asked that the proposed agent, who waited in an ante-room, might be presented. In a moment the chamberlain announced our old friend Isidorus. With bowed head and hands folded upon his breast, he stood on the threshhold, and then advancing, knelt gracefully before the Empress. He evidently made a good impression, for her Majesty smiled graciously and said :—

"It is a difficult quest on which I would send thee, but thou shalt be well rewarded for thy fidelity and zeal."

"My humble services, my life, are at your Majesty's disposal," said the Greek. "I shall deem myself well rewarded by your Majesty's favour."

"See'st thou this lady ?" asked the Empress, pointing to Callirhoë. "To find her sire in this wide world—that is thy task ;" and she briefly explained the nature of the commission.

The youth gazed long and earnestly on the fair face of the girl, and replied, "Those features once seen can never be forgotten. If I find anywhere on earth aught resembling them, I shall not fail to recognize the likeness. In such a quest I would gladly search the wide world over."

"My chamberlain will amply equip you for
your journey, and will give you a letter, with the
Emperor's seal, to all the Roman prefects in
Italy; and, by the Divine favour, I trust you
will bring us good tidings."

"So may it be," said the youth, as he retired
from the presence, giving, as he did so, a lingering
look at Callirhoë, who, with dilated eyes and
parted lips, gazed at him with an intensity of
entreaty that would have proved an inspiration
to a less susceptible nature than his.

CHAPTER X.

A WICKED PLOT.

WE have already mentioned the fact that Fausta, the mother of the Emperor Galerius, was a fanatical pagan. The especial object of her regard was the goddess Cybele, who was worshipped in Rome with rites of the most degrading superstition. Fausta was intensely bitter in her hatred of the Christian name, and strenuously endeavoured to incite her son, the Emperor, to persecution. She was especially virulent towards her daughter-in-law, the beautiful Valeria, and sought by every means to embitter the mind of Galerius against her. In this she was strongly abetted, or rather inspired, by Furca, the vicious old priest of Cybele, whose wicked influence over her was very great. This worthy pair, the day after the interview above described, were engaged in a secret conclave or conspiracy against Valeria and the

Christians, while the latter was seeking to carry out her benevolent enterprise.

The scene of their interview was the reception-room of Fausta, in the palace of the Emperor Galerius. It was far more sumptuously furnished and decorated than that of the Empress Valeria, and at one end, in a marble niche, stood an ugly image of the goddess Cybele, with her crown of many towers, rudely carved out of olive wood, but quite embrowned, and almost blackened with age. It was bedizened with costly jewels, and was deemed to be of special sanctity. Before it was a small marble altar, on which burned, day and night, a silver censer.

At the moment of which we write, Fausta approached the altar, and kissing her hand to the image—an ancient mode of worship, from which we get the word "adore"—she took some costly Sabean incense from a small gold coffer, and sprinkled it on the glowing coals of the censer. Dense white fumes arose, whose rich aromatic odour filled the large apartment. Fausta had been an Illyrian peasant, and, notwithstanding her embroidered robes and costly jewels, she still exhibited much of the rude peasant character and lack of culture. Her coarse and wrinkled features and swarthy complexion, were all the more striking by their contrast with the snowy mantle, with its gold-embroidered border, which she wore; and her bright black eyes glittered with an expression of deadly malice like those of a serpent. While she stood before the altar, a servant announced that Furca, the arch-priest of Cybele, had obeyed her summons. As the curtain of the door was drawn aside, a little weazened old man, as dark as mahogany, wearing a thick crop of snow white hair, appeared.

"Thanks, good Furca," said Fausta, "I desire your counsel on a matter of much importance to the State, and to the worship of the holy Cybele."

"At your service, your Excellency," said the obsequious priest, who also kissed his hand to the black-faced image, and sprinkled a few grains of incense on the censer.

"Thou knowest how the worship of the Galilean Christus has increased, not only among the common people, the vile plebs, and the still viler slave population, but even among the patricians and nobles. I have evidence that even in this palace, and very near the throne, the execrable superstition is cherished.

"Alas! your Excellency, I fear it is only too true," whined the bigot arch-priest. "Certain it is that neither of the Empresses, Prisca or Valeria, ever take part in the public worship of

the gods, as from their lofty station it is their
duty to do."

"Yes, and I have reason to believe that there
is plotting and conniving between the Empress
and the accursed Christian sect."

"Hast any proof of this?" asked the arch-
priest, eagerly. "This is a crime against the
State."

"The black slave Juba," replied Fausta, "is, as
thou knowest, a faithful worshipper of Cybele,
and she told me even now, that Adauctus, the
Imperial Treasurer, had been only yesterday
closeted with the Empress, and plotting to restore
to the favour of the Emperor a certain Demetrius,
a Christian renegade, who is in hiding for his
crimes."

"Oh, ho!" chuckled the priest, with a wicked
grin, my fine lady need not think herself so high
and mighty as to be above the reach of the law,
or beyond the anger of the insulted gods."

"I would almost give my eyes," hissed through
her teeth the revengeful Fausta, "if I could only
see that painted doll, Valeria, abased and degraded.
She has too long held a sway, of which I, the
mother of the Emperor, have been deprived."

"I trust you may not only see it," said Furca,
gloating in anticipation over the prospect, "but
also see her pale, proud mother, the Empress
Prisca, humbled at your feet."

"Accomplish this," good Furca," exclaimed
Fausta, with exultation, "and the goddess Cybele
shall have such an offering as she never had
before."

"We must be wary," said the priest, "or we
may ourselves be crushed. They are too powerful to be attacked openly. We must plot
against them secretly. I'll be a *furca* to them
indeed," he added, punning upon his own name,
which had also the signification of an instrument
of punishment, something like a cross; and the
conspirators parted with this pledge of mutual
hate against their destined victims.

CHAPTER XI.

THE SLAVE MARKET.

IN the meantime Isidorus, with well-filled purse, and armed with credentials under the Imperial seal, had set off upon his difficult and doubtful quest."

"However it turn out," he said to himself, "it will be strange if I do not climb a few steps higher on the ladder on which my feet are now placed. Being the confidential agent of the Empress is better than being the secretary of the rude soldier, Sertorius, and being snubbed by him every day, too."

Mounted on one of the best horses in the Imperial stables, he rode forth upon the famous Salarian Way, which led straight as an arrow over the wide Campagna, and over the rugged Appenines to the distant city of Ravenna, among the marshes of the Adriatic. Now a decayed and grass-grown city, six miles from the sea, it

was then a great and busy port, and had been for
two centuries and a half an important see of the
Christian Church.   Not to the prefect of the
city, but to the bishop of Ravenna, Isidorus,
with his natural tact and shrewdness, betook
himself. The sign manual of the Emperor, which
he confidently exhibited, did not command that
regard which he had anticipated; but a private
letter from Adauctus, commending Isidorus to
all Christian bishops and presbyters, procured
for him a much more cordial reception.   He
was hospitably entertained, and every possible
assistance given him in his quest. The bishop
called together the deacons who had the care of
the poor of the Church, but none of them knew
anything of Demetrius. The bishop had ransomed many Christian slaves—prisoners taken in
war, or captured by pirates. A few years before,
when the resources of the Church had been
completely exhausted by the exercise of this
charity,* a company of captives had been sold by
pirates to a Jewish slave-dealer named Ezra, and
conveyed by him to the city of Mediolanum, or
as we now call it, Milan, as offering, next to

---

* This might easily happen, for after successful raids
or slave hunts, the victims were sold by their pirate
captors by the thousand. The fact is on record, that at
Delos, a famous slave market, 60,000 were sold by
Celician pirates in a single day.

Rome, the best market for his wares. And one of the deacons remembered among this slave-gang an old man who resembled the description given of Demetrius.

To Milan, therefore, crossing again the Appenines, and riding up the broad, rich valley of the Po, went Isidorus. He was surprised to find a city, almost rivalling in extent Rome itself, and with a history reaching back to the times of the Etruscans, well-nigh a thousand years. First he sought the Jewish slave-dealer, who kept a regular mart for the sale or hire of human beings, just as one now-a-days keeps a livery-stable for the sale or hire of horses. There was as much fraud, too, in selling slaves then, as has been proverbially connected with horse-dealing and jockeying in every age. The *ergastulum*, or slave-pen of Ezra, was a large prison-like structure, surrounding the four sides of a hollow square. There were no windows to the street, and only very small iron-grated ones to the inner court; with heavy, iron-studded doors to the stable-like stalls, where the slaves were chained to a stout beam running along the wall.

A slave-auction was in progress when Isidorus arrived, so he had to wait till it was over before plying his quest. A gang of slaves, unchained, but guarded by keepers, armed with whips and spears, awaited their fate. Stripped nearly naked, they were rudely examined, pinched, handled, and made to stoop, lift heavy weights, walk, run, and show their paces like horses for sale. Many had their ears bored—a sign of servitude from the time of Moses—and others were seamed with scars of the cruel lash. This, however, lessened their market value, as it was evidence of their intractable and troublesome character.

Slavery was, at the time of which we write, one of the greatest evils of the Roman empire. It was a deadly canker, eating out the national life. It cast a stigma of disgrace on labour, and prevented the formation of that intelligent middle class which is the true safeguard of liberty. Never in the history of the world was society so based upon the abject misery of vast multitudes of human beings. The slaves outnumbered, many times, their masters. They were forbidden to wear a peculiar garb, lest they should recognize their numbers and their strength, and rise in universal revolt. As it was, servile insurrections were of frequent occurrence. But they were crushed and punished with ruthless severity. In one slave revolt, 60,000 of these wretched beings were slain. The first question about a man's property was, " *Quot pascit servos?*"—" How many slaves does he keep ? " Ten was considered the least number consistent with any degree of respectability. Four hundred slaves deluged with their blood the funeral pyre of Pedanius Secundus. Vidius Pollio fed his lampreys with the bodies of his human chattels. A single freedman left over 4,000 at his death. Some 2,000 men were lords of the Roman world, and the great mass of the rest were slaves. Their condition was one of inconceivable wretchedness. They had no rights of marriage, nor any claim to their children. Their food was a pound of bread a day, with a little salt and oil. Flesh they never tasted, and even wine, which flowed like water, almost never. Colossal piles, built by their blood and sweat, attest to the present day the bitterness of their bondage. The lash of the taskmaster was heard in the fields, and crosses, bearing aloft their quivering victims, polluted the wayside.

This dumb, weltering mass of humanity, crushed by power, and led by their lusts, became a hot-bed of vice, in which every evil passion grew apace. To these wretched beings came the gospel of liberty, with a strange, a thrilling power. The oppressed slave, in the intervals of toil or torture, caught with joy the emancipating message, and sprang up enfranchised by an immortalizing hope. He exulted in a new-found freedom in Christ, which no wealth could purchase, no chains of slavery fetter, nor even death itself destroy. In the Christian Church the

distinctions of worldly rank were abolished.*
The highest spiritual privileges were opened to
the lowliest slave.   In the ecclesiastical hierarchy
were no rights of birth, and no privileges of
blood.   In the inscriptions of the Catacombs, no
badges of servitude, no titles of honour appear.
The wealthy noble, the lord of many acres,
recognized in his lowly servant a fellow heir
of glory.   They bowed together at the same
table of the Lord, saluted each other with the
mutual kiss of charity, and side by side in their
narrow graves, at length returned to indistinguish-
able dust.   The story of Onesimus was often
repeated, and the patrician master received his
returning slave, "not now as a servant, but
above a servant—a brother beloved."   Nay, he
may even have bowed to him as his ecclesiastical
superior, and received from his plebeian hands
the emblems of their common Lord.

We return from this digression to the slave-
market of Milan.   Very few of Ezra's stock were
black—not more than half a dozen, from Nubia
and Libya.   Most of them were as white as
himself, or whiter still.   There were Dalmatians,
Illyrians, Iberians, Gauls, Greeks, Syrians, and
many other nationalities.   Ezra was engaged

---

* Apud nos inter pauperes et divites, servos et
dominos, interest nihiL Lactant. *Div. Inst.* v. 14, 15.

in busy converse, in a broken mixture of Latin and Greek, with the wealthy patrician, Vitellius, the lord of wide corn lands on the fertile banks of the Po.

"Field hands your Excellency wants? I have some splendid ones," he said, eagerly. "Here, you fellows, step out there and show your muscles;" and he struck with his whip-lash two brawny white-skinned, blue-eyed, yellow-haired British slaves.

"Sullen dogs these British often are," he said, "but they are as good as gold. They never run away like the Germans, nor steal like the Greeks, nor kill themselves like the Gauls."*

"Glad of that," said Vitellius. "I have had a perfect epidemic of suicide among my slaves. I had to kill several of them to keep them from killing themselves"—a sad but frequent comment on the utter wretchedness of their condition, from which death itself was the only refuge.

"Does your Excellency want anything of a higher grade?" asked Ezra. "Some skilled workmen to finish your elegant villa, for instance. I have a splendid Greek sculptor, almost another Phidias, and another a second Zeuxis with the

* These were the most common faults of slaves, for attempting which they were often branded on cheek or brow.

brush. Then if you want a steward, or book-keeper, or secretary, or reader, or a skilled physician, I have them all; or a hand-maid for your Excellency's wife. I have a beautiful Greek girl here, highly accomplished; can embroider, play the zither, sing in two languages. I sold her sister last week for 100,000 sesterces* —nieces of an ex-archon. I felt really sorry for them, but what would you?—trade is trade. Times are bad. Poor Ezra has had bad luck. Several of his slaves kill themselves. Market glutted; price falls. I sell them very cheap—very cheap."

Vitellius made his purchases, had them chained together in a gang, and driven by his steward, like cattle, to his farm. The account of Ezra's interview with Isidorus we must defer to another chapter.

---

* Over $4,000 of our money. Very beautiful or accomplished slaves sometimes brought twice that amount.

CHAPTER XII.

THE LOST FOUND.

"DO you remember buying or selling a slave named Demetrius, a Jew?" asked Isidorus of Ezra, the slave-dealer of Milan. He wasted no words in circumlocution, for he knew that there was no use in trying to deceive the keen-eyed Jewish dealer in his fellow-man; and that his best chances of success were in coming directly to the point.

"Selling a Jew? Oh, no! I never sell my own kinsmen. That's against our law. It is like seething a kid in its mother's milk. I often ransom them from pirates and set them free."

"But this Demetrius was a Christian Jew—a convert from Moses to Jesus," said the Greek.

"A Christian dog," cried Ezra with a wicked execration. "He was no Jew. He had sold his birthright like Esau, and had no part nor

lot with Israel. Of course, I'd sell him if I
got him—to the mines, or to the galleys, or
the field gang, to the hardest master I could
find. But I know naught about your Demetrius,
who was he ?"

"He was a Jew of Antioch," said Isidorus,
" captured by Illyrian pirates and sold in the
slave market of Ravenna."

"That is a common tale," replied Ezra."
There are many such. How long since this
occurred ?"

" 'Tis now five years since he was last seen
by her who seeks him, and who will pay well
for his recovery."

"Just my luck," grumbled the greedy Jew.
" Some one else will gain the prize. 'Tis not
for me."

" Then you cannot help me in this quest ?"
said the Greek.

" How can I remember the scores and hundreds of Christian dogs that I have bought
and sold ? Go ask these monks, they know
more of the vermin than I do."

Acting on this hint, Isidorus made his way
to the Convent of San Lorenzo, the ancient
chapel of which still remains. Knocking at
a bronze-studded gateway he was admitted to
a quadrangle surrounded by cloisters or covered
galleries upon which opened the doors of the

different apartments. It was more like a hospital and alms-house than like what is now understood as a convent. It served as a sort of school of theology, youthful acolytes and deacons being here trained for the office and work of presbyters in the Church. Isidorus presented his letter from Adauctus to the good Bishop Paulinus, and was most cordially received.

"Right welcome art thou, my son," said the bishop, "bearing, as thou dost, the commendation of the worthy Adauctus; and right glad shall we be to promote thy search. I myself know naught that can throw light upon it, inasmuch as I lived not at Milan, but was bishop of Nola at the time of which thou speakest."

The scriptor, or secretary, of the convent was also consulted without avail, no record being found in the annals of the house that gave any hope of discovery.

"Come lunch with us in the refectory," said the bishop, "and I will ask if any of the brethren know aught of this mystery."

The refectory was a large bare-looking room —its only furniture being a long and solid table with a shorter one across the end for the bishop, and presbyters, and visitors. Of this latter there were frequently several, as such houses were the chief places for entertaining the travelling clergy or even lay members of the Christian brotherhood. Upon the walls were certain somewhat grim-looking frescoes, representing Biblical scenes and characters like those in the Catacombs described in chapter VIII. At one side of the room was a *bema*, or reading-desk, at which one of the lectors—a distinct ecclesiastical office,* with its special ordination —read, while the brethren partook of their meals, the lessons for the day from the Gospels and Epistles, as well as passages from the writings of Clement, Ignatius, Justin Martyr, and Origen. For this usage the scarcity and high price of MS. books, and the desire to improve every moment of time was deemed a sufficient ground.

After the meal—which was almost ascetic in its simplicity, consisting chiefly of vegetable pottage, lentils, and bread—was over, and the reading ended, the bishop explained the cause of the presence among them of a stranger from Rome.

"My brethren," he said in conclusion, "this

---

* This office was possibly derived from the synagogue. As requiring good scholarship it was one of much honour, and was even sought by laymen. The Emperor Julian, in his youth, and his brother Gallus, were readers in the Church of Nicomedia. Many epitaphs of readers occur in the Catacombs.

is a common story. Many are the victims of cruelty and wrong in this great empire. Be it ours, so far as God may give us power, to succour the oppressed and redress their wrongs."

As he sat down a venerable presbyter rose and said, "Father, five years have I been under this hospitable roof, ransomed from bondage by your predecessor in office. Five years have I mourned the loss of a son and daughter, sold from my arms to I know not what cruel fate. It may be that God is about to restore me my children, the flesh of my flesh. Hast thou, O stranger, any sign or token by which I may be assured of their identity?"

"Of thy son I have no tidings; but know thou if this be a token of thy daughter's rescue," and Isidorus exhibited the small cornelian *tessara* of the fish of which we have spoken.

Eagerly the old man clasped it, and scanned the inscription, and joyfully exclaimed, while tears of gladness flowed down his aged cheeks and silvery beard, "Thank God, my child yet lives. I shall again behold her before I die. See, here is her very name, 'Callirhoë, daughter of Demetrius.' I carved it with my own hands one happy day in our dear home in Damascus. God is good. I never hoped to see her again. Tell me, stranger, is she, too, a slave?"

"Nay," said Isidorus with emotion, for even

his careless nature was touched with sympathy at the joy of the old man, "She is the freed woman of the Empress Valeria, and high in favour, too, I should judge, from the interest her august mistress showed in seeking for thee."

"*Benedic, anima mea, Domino,*" exclaimed the aged presbyter with fervour, "*et omnia, quae intra me sunt, nomini sacro ejus*—Bless the Lord, O my soul: and all that is within me bless His holy name. He hath heard my prayer. He hath answered my supplication."

The old man's story was soon told. He had been rescued from the slave pen of Ezra, and employed in the service of the convent. His familiar knowledge of Greek led to his appointment as instructor in that language of the young acolytes and deacons who were in training for the office of the ministry. At length his superior gifts and fervent piety led to his own ordination as a presbyter of the Church of Milan.

CHAPTER XIII.

FATHER AND DAUGHTER.

DEMETRIUS was now eager to set out for Rome to behold once more the child whom he had scarce hoped ever to see again. A happy leave-taking of the brethren of Milan, who rejoiced in fraternal sympathy, followed; and on a gently ambling mule, at break of day, the old man rode forth beside the gallantly equipped Isidorus. He beguiled the weary way with questions about his long-lost daughter, as to her growth, appearance, her apparent health, and even the very garb she wore. He was never tired hearing about her, and recounting incidents of her childhood and youth. The only shadow upon his joy was the vague mystery concerning the fate of his son. But he said cheerfully: "God is good. He has restored to me one of my children. I feel confident that in His own good time He will restore also the other."

Beneath the fatigue of the long journey of nearly three hundred miles his powers would have failed, had he not been inspirited and sustained by the thrilling anticipation of beholding once more his beloved child.

At length, near sunset, on the tenth day, they drew near the great metropolis of the Empire. Clearer and clearer to the view rose the seven-hilled city's pride, the snowy marble peristyles and pediments of palace and temple, gleaming in the rosy light like transparent alabaster. To the left rose the cliff-like walls of the Colosseum, even then venerable with the time-stains of over two hundred years. In the foreground stretched the long Aurelian Wall, with its towers and battlements and strong arched gates. They crossed the Tiber by the Milvian Bridge, built three hundred years before, and destined to witness within ten years that fierce struggle for the mastery of the empire, between Constantine and Maxentius, when the British-born Cæsar saw, or thought he saw, in the mid-day heavens a blazing cross, and exclaiming "By this sign we conquer," overwhelmed his adversary in the rushing river.*

Passing under the hill crowned with the

---

* A magnificent painting in the Vatican represents with vivid realism this scene, the drowning of the Pagan Emperor, and the defeat and flight of all his army.

famous gardens of Lucullus, now known as the
Pincio, and beneath the heavy-arched gateway
in the wall, they made their way through the
narrow streets towards the centre of the city
—the Forum and the Palatine. It was a day
of festival—the last day of the *Quinquatria,*
or festival of Minerva. Garlands of flowers,
and wreaths of laurel, festooned many of the
houses, in front of which blazed coloured cressets
and lamps. Sacred processions were passing
through the streets, with torches and music
and chantings of priests ; and eyer and anon
the shrill blare of the sacred trumpets pierced
the ear of night. In the Forum the temples
of Saturn, and of Castor, and Pollux were
richly adorned and brilliantly illuminated, and
a great throng of merry-makers filled the
marble square.

Turning to the left, our travellers ascended
the slope of the Palatine Hill, amid ever-
increasing grandeur of architecture. Demetrius,
though he had travelled far and seen much,
was struck with astonishment at the splendour
and magnificence of the buildings. Not at
Jerusalem, or Damascus, or Antioch, not at
Ravenna or Milan, had he witnessed such wealth
of porphyry and marble, such stately colonades
and peristyles, covering acres of ground—now
but a mound of mouldering ruins.

8

"Whither art thou leading me?" asked
Demetrius, as they stood before a palace of
snowy marble which, bathed in the mellow
radiance of the rising moon, seemed transformed
into translucent alabaster.

"To the abode where dwells thy daughter,
the favoured freed-woman of the mistress of all
this splendour," replied Isidorus, enjoying the
wonder and admiration of his companion in
travel.

A fountain splashed in the centre of the
square, its waters flashing like silver in the
moonlight. The burnished mail of the Roman
soldiers gleamed as the guard was changed, and
their armour clashed as they grounded their
spears and saluted the officer of the watch.

"What, Max, are you on duty to-night?" said
Isidorus as he recognized a soldier of the guard.
"Any promotion in your service yet?"

"No, but I see that there is in yours," said
the bluff out-spoken guardsman.

"Well, yes, I flatter myself that there is,"
replied the vain-glorious Greek, "and I hope for
still more."

Announcing to the chamberlain of the palace
that he had just arrived from a journey of
important business for the Empress Valeria, he
with Demetrius were taken to a marble bath,
where with the aid of a skilful slave, they made

their toilet for immediate presentation to the Empress.

Valeria was attended as usual by her freed-woman Callirhoë, when the Greek was announced.

"We heard," she said to Isidorus, "by thy letters, of the failure of thy quest at Ravenna and Milan, but we hope—— "

At this moment, with an exclamation of intensest emotion Callirhoë rushed forward and flung herself in the arms of the venerable figure who had followed the Greek into the apartment.

"My father!" she cried in tones which thrilled every heart, and then she embraced him again and again. The impassioned love and joy and gratitude of her soul struggling for expression, she burst into a flood of tears.

"My daughter, child of my beloved Rachel," exclaimed the old man, as, heedless of the presence of the Empress, he fondly caressed her, "do I again embrace thee ?   Thou art the very image of thy angel-mother, as I first beheld her in the rose gardens of Sharon. Truly God is good. Now, Lord, lettest thou thy servant depart in peace—the cup of my happiness runneth over."

"Nay, good father," broke in the soft voice of the Empress, who was deeply moved by the scene, "rather live to share thy daughter's love and happiness."

"Pardon, august lady," said Demetrius, falling on his knees, and gratefully kissing the Empress's hand. "Pardon, that in the joy of finding my child I forgot the duty I owe to my sovereign."

"Thy first duty was there," said Valeria, pointing to the lovely Callirhoë, who, smiling through her tears, was now leaning on her father's arm. "We leave you to exchange your mutual confidences. Good Isidorus it shall be our care to bestow a reward commensurate with thy merit;" and she withdrew to her own apartment.

"My everlasting gratitude thou hast," said Callirhoë, with her sweetest smile, frankly extending her hand.

"I am, indeed, well repaid," said the Greek, as he respectfully kissed it. "I would gladly show my zeal in much more arduous service," and bowing low, he was accompanied by the chamberlain to the vestibule. That official gave him, by command of the Empress, a purse of gold, and assured him of still further reward.

CHAPTER XIV.

"UNSTABLE AS WATER."

IT was with feelings highly elated at his successful achievement, which presaged still further advancement, that Isidorus sought his lodgings. On the way he met many late revellers returning from the festival, "flown with insolence and wine," and making night hideous with their riot. Among them, his garments dishevelled, and a withering garland falling from his brow, was an old acquaintance, Calphurnius, the son of the Perfect, who with maudlin affection embraced him and exclaimed:—

"Friend of my soul, where hast thou hidden thyself? Our wine parties lack half their zest, since thou hast turned anchorite. Come, pledge our ancient friendship in a goblet of Falernian. The wine shop of Turbo, the ex-gladiator, is near at hand.

"You have not turned Christian, have you?"

hiccoughed the drunken reveller; "no offence, but I heard you had, you know."

Isidorus gave a start. Were his visits to the Catacomb known to this fashionable fop? Were they a matter of sport to him and his boon companions? Was he to be laughed out of his nascent convictions by these empty-headed idlers? No, he determined. He despised the whole crew. But he was not the stuff out of which martyrs are made, and he lacked the courage to confess to this gilded butterfly, his as yet faltering feeling towards Christianity.

"Who says I am?" he asked, anxious to test his knowledge on the subject.

"Who says so? I don't know. Why everybody," was the rather vague reply.

"You don't know what you are talking about, man," said the Greek, with a forced laugh. "Go home and sleep off your carouse."

"All right. I told them so. The Christians, indeed, the vermin! Come to the Baths of Caracalla at noon to-morrow and I'll tell you all about it."

Isidorus went to his lodgings and retired to his couch, but not to slumber. He was like a boat drifting rudderless upon the sea, the sport of every wind that blew. He had no strength of will, no fixedness of purpose, no depth of conviction. His susceptible disposition

was easily moved to generous impulses and even
to noble aspirations, yet he had no moral
firmness. He is portrayed to the life by the
words of the great Teacher, "He that received
the seed into stony places, the same is he that
heareth the Word, and anon, with joy receiveth
it; yet hath he not root in himself, but dureth
for a while; for when tribulation or persecution
ariseth because of the ' Word, bye-and-bye he
is offended."

"Did his boon companions," he questioned,
"suspect that any serious convictions had penetrated beneath his light and careless exterior ?"
All his good resolutions had begun like wax
in a furnace to melt and give way at the
sneer and jeer of the shallow fool from whom
he had just parted—a creature whom in his
inmost heart he despised. Strange contradiction
of human nature ! Like the epicurean poet,
he saw and approved the better way and yet
he followed the worse.* He seemed to gain
in the few casual words he had heard, a glimpse
of the possibilities of persecution which menaced
him if faithful to his convictions, and he had
not moral fibre enough to encounter them. And
yet his conscience stung and tortured him as
he tossed upon his restless couch. Toward

* Video, proboque meliora,
  Deterioraque sequor.—*Hor.*

morning he fell asleep and it was broad day when he awoke. His reflections were as different from those with which he fell asleep as the brilliant daylight was from the gloomy shadows of night. The air was full of the busy hum of life. Water sellers and fruit pedlers and the like were crying "*Aqua Gelata*," "Fresh Figs," and "White wine and red." Cohorts of soldiers were clattering in squadrons, through the streets, the sunlight glittering on their spearpoints and on the bosses of their shields and armour. Jet black Nubian slaves, clad in snowy white, were bearing in gold-adorned *lecticæ* or palanquins, proud patrician dames, robed in saffron and purple, to visit the shops of the jewellers and silk mercers. Senators and civic officials were flocking to the Forum with their murmuring crowd of clients. Gilded youths were hastening to the schools of the rhetoricians or of the gladiators, both alike deemed necessary instructors of these pinks of fashion. The streets and squares were a perfect kaleidoscope of colour and movement— an eddying throng, on business or on pleasure bent.

The stir and animation of the scene dispelled all serious thoughts from the mind of the frivolous Greek. He plunged like a strong swimmer into the stream of eager busy life surging through the streets. He was one of the gayest of the gay, ready with his laugh and joke as he met his youthful comrades.

"Ho, Rufus, whither away in such mad haste," he cried as he saw a young officer of the 12th Legion dashing past in his chariot, driving with admirable skill two milk-white steeds through the crowded streets.

"Oh! are you there? Where have you hidden yourself for the last month?" exclaimed Rufus, as he sharply reined up his steeds. "To the Baths of Caracalla; will you go?"

"Yes, very gladly," said Isidorus, stepping upon the low platform of the open bronze chariot. "I have been beyond the Po, on a special service—a barbarous region. No baths, circus, or games like those of Rome."

"There is but one Rome," said the fiery young Hotspur, "but I am beginning to hate it. I am fairly rusting with idleness and long for active service—whether amid Libyian sands or Pannonian forests, I care not."

"It seems to me," replied the effeminate Greek, "that I could console myself with your horses and chariot—the coursers of Achilles were not more swift—and with the delights which Rome and its fair dames are eager to lavish on that favourite of fortune, Ligurius Rufus."

"*Vanitas vanitatis*," yawned the youth. "Life

is a tremendous bore. I was made for action, for conquest, for state craft; but under this despotism of the Cæsars, we are all slaves together. You and I fare a little better than that Nubian porter yonder, that is all."

"Yet you seem to bear your bondage very comfortably," laughed the light-hearted Greek, "and had I your fortune, so would I."

"Mehercule! the fetters gall though they be golden," ejaculated the soldier, lashing his steeds into swifter flight, as if to give vent to his nervous excitement. "I plunge into folly to forget that I am a slave. Lost a hundred thousand sesterees at dice last night. The empire is hurrying to chaos. There are no paths of honour and ambition open to a man. One must crouch like a hound or crawl like a serpent to win advancement in the state. I tell you the degenerate Romans of to-day are an effete and worn out race. The rude Dacians beyond the Tiber possess more of the hardy virtues of the founders of the Republic than the craven creatures who crawl about the feet of the modern Colossi, who bestride the world and are worshipped almost as gods. And unless Rome mends her ways they will be the masters of the Empire yet."

"One would think you were Cato the Censor," laughed the Greek. "For my part, I think the best philosophy is that of my wise countryman, Epicurus—'to take the times as they come, and make the most of them.' But here we are at the Thermæ."

Giving his horses to one of the innumerable grooms belonging to the establishment, Rufus and his friend disappeared under the lofty arched entrance of the stately Baths of Caracalla.

CHAPTER XV

AT THE BATHS.

NOTHING can give one a more striking conception of Roman life under the Empire than the size, number, and magnificence of the public baths. Those of Caracalla are a typical example. They oovered an area of fifteen hundred by twelve hundred and fifty feet, the surrounding grounds being a mile in circumference. They formed a perfect wilderness of stately halls, and corridors, and chambers, the very mouldering remains of which strike one with astonishment. Of this very structure, the poet Shelley, in the preface of his "Prometheus Unbound," remarks: "This poem was chiefly written upon the mountainous ruins of the Baths of Caracalla, among the flowery glades and thickets of odoriferous blossoming trees, which are extended in ever-widening labyrinths upon its immense platforms, and dizzy arches suspended in the air." Piers of sold masonry soar aloft like towers, on the summit of which good-sized trees are growing. Climbing one of those massive towers, the present writer enjoyed a glorious sunset-view of the mighty maze, of the crumbling ruins which rose like stranded wrecks above the sea of verdure all around, and of the far spreading and desolate Campagna.

The great hypocausts, or subterranean furnaces, can be still examined, as also the caleducts in the walls for hot air, and the metal pipes for hot and cold water. The baths were supplied by an aqueduct constructed for that purpose, the arches of which may be seen bestriding the Campagna for a distance of fourteen miles from the city. There were hot, and cold, and tepid baths, *caldaria*, or sweating chambers, *frigidaria*, or cooling rooms, *unctoria*, or anointing rooms, and many others sufficient to accommodate sixteen hundred bathers at once. There were also a vast gymnasium for exercise, a *stadium*, or race-course, and a *pinacotheca*, or art gallery. Here were found the famous Farnese Bull, the largest group of ancient statuary extant, and many *chefs d'œuvre* of classic sculpture and mosaics.

The Baths of Diocletian, built by the labours of the Christians during the last great persecution, one authority says, were twice as large, and could accommodate eighteen thousand bathers in a day, but that seems incredible. One of its great halls, a hundred yards by thirty in area, and thirty yards high, was converted by Michael Angelo into a church. Of the remainder, part is used as a monastery, part as barracks, and part as an orphanage, a poor-house, and an asylum for the blind, and much is in ruins. At Pompeii is a public bath in perfect preservation, with the niches for the clothing, soaps, and unguents of the bathers, and even the *strigils*, or bronze instruments for scraping the skin—the same after eighteen hundred years as though used but yesterday. By these means we are able to reconstruct the outward circumstances of that old Roman life, almost as though we had shared its busy movement.

As Ligurius Rufus drew aside the heavy matting of the doorway of the Thermæ, of Caracalla, which then, as now, kept out the summer heat from the buildings of Rome, a busy scene burst upon his view. A great hall, lighted by openings in the roof, was filled with gay groups of patrician Romans, sauntering, chatting, laughing, exchanging news, betting on the next races, and settling bets on the last. As the modern clubman goes to his club to see the papers and learn the current gossip, so all the idlers in Rome came to the baths as to a social exchange, to learn the latest bit of court scandal or public news.

"Ho, Calphurnius!" said Rufus, to the now sobered son of the city Prefect; "what's in the wind to-day? You know all the mischief that's going."

"Sorry I cannot maintain my reputation then. Things are dull as an old *strigil*. Oh, by the way," and he beckoned them into a recess behind a porphyry pillar, "there is going to be a precious row up at the palace. I tell you in confidence. The old vixen, Fausta, has got a new spite against the Empress Valeria, whom all the people of the palace love. The termagant is not fit to carry water for her bath. She has found some mare's nest of a Christian plot,—by the way you are mixed up in it, friend Isidorus. I would advise you to have a care. In the fight of Pagan against Christian, I fear Valeria will get the worst of it, *dii avertant.*"

"The palace walls are not glass," laughed Isidorus, "nor have you a Dionysius' ear. How know you all this?"

"As if the Roman Prefect did not know what goes on, that he thinks worth knowing, in every house in Rome! He has eyes and ears in his pay everywhere; and when honest Juba, or Tubal, come with their secret intelligence, they are not above accepting double pay and letting me into the secret, too. Besides that crafty old vulture Furca was closeted with the Prefect for an hour by the clepshydra, and you always smell carrion when he is hovering round."

" What is it all about ? " asked Rufus. " I am sure Valeria is as much beloved by the people as the old termagant Fausta is hated."

" There's the rub—a bit of spiteful jealousy," answered Calphurnius. " But when that old basilisk hates, she will find a way to sting."

" But what have I to do with the quarrels of the palace? " asked Isidorus, a little anxiously, for he knew not how far he might be compromised by the commission he had executed, of which he had felt not a little proud.

" You know best yourself," answered Calphurnius with a laugh. " If you have done a service to Valeria or the Christians, you have made an enemy of Fausta and the Pagans."

" Is this what you spoke of last night, and promised to explain to-day ? " asked the Greek.

" Yes, I suppose so. I have no very distinct recollection of what I said. I had been supping with Rufus here, and some other roystering blades, and the Folernian was uncommonly good. Come, *amicus meus*," he went on turning to Ligurius, " don't you want revenge for those sesterces you lost last night ? "

" I don't mind if I do punish you a little," yawned the young soldier. " It will kill the time for awhile, at all events."

CHAPTER XVI.

THE GAMING TABLE.

GAMING was a perfect passion among the Romans, and indeed among most ancient nations. Dice of bone and ivory, like those in use to-day, have been found in the tombs of Thebes and Luxor. Æschylus and Sophocles describe their use four hundred years before Christ, and in an ancient Greek picture now before us, a female figure is shown tossing *tali*, or gaming cubes, and catching them on the back of her hand, as children now play "Jacks." Soldiers from the enforced idleness of much of their time and the intense excitement of the rest of it, have in every age been addicted to gambling to beguile the *ennui* of their too ample leisure—from those of Alexander down to the raw recruits of to-day. Our friend, Ligurius Rufus, had undergone frequent experience of the pains and pleasures of this siren vice; but

9

was eager to return to its embrace. Such vast
estates had been squandered, and great families
impoverished, and large fortunes often staked
upon a single throw of the dice—beyond anything
that Homburg or Monaco ever saw — that
gambling was forbidden by successive Roman
laws. But when were not the rich able to
indulge in their favourite vices, even under a
much purer Government than that of Rome?
So even in this place of public resort, were
numerous alcoves in which stood gaming tables,
while money changers—generally Jews—had
tables near for giving good Roman sesterces
in exchange for the *oboloi* or *drachmai* of Greece,
the shekels of Jerusalem, or the scarabæus coins
of Egypt. Into one of these alcoves the three
friends now turned, Isidorus promising himself
that he would only look on. He had been
excessively addicted to play, but had, notwithstanding occasional success, lost so much money
that he had abjured the seductive vice, especially
since his visit to the Catacomb with his friend
Faustus, who had urged him to forsake a practice
so perilous in itself, and so opposed to Christian
conduct.

Calphurnius and Rufus sat down to the gaming
table, and the Greek stood looking on. The
gold was placed in two piles on the board. The
dice rattled, and eager eyes took in at a glance

the number of red spots on the upper surface. Rufus seemed to have recovered his good fortune. Throw after throw was successful.

"That is the *Jactus Venereus*," he exclaimed with exultation, as he made the cast that counted highest. "We must have wine and I must be toast-master," for so was called the leader of the revels.

The Greek watched with honest interest the play, his eye flashing and his pulse quickening under its strange spell. The richest wines of Chios and Lesbos were ordered; and as the wine was poured into jewelled goblets, he required slight urging to partake of the fragrant vintage of the Isles of Greece. The eager play was resumed. The Greek noted each practised turn of the wrist and cast of the dice—his eye kindling and his brain throbbing with the subtle intoxication of both the game and the wine.

"I've won enough," said Rufus, "I've got back my own, and more. I don't want to ruin you, my good fellow," and he positively declined to play any more. His honest nature recoiled from taking that for which he gave no value, beyond recouping his previous losses.

"Will you try a cast," he added, turning to Isidorus. "Our friend has lots of money to lose?" and he lounged away to watch the game of ball in the Gymnasium.

"Yes, take a turn, my luck is wretched to-day!"
exclaimed Calphurnius. "Come, I will stake
that pile of gold on a single cast."

The Greek's whole frame was tingling with
excitement—yet he was withheld by some lingering restraint of his promise to Faustus to abandon
play. Calphurnius again rattled the dice, the
cast was a complete blank—the worst possible
combination.

"'Twas lucky for me you were not playing
then," he said, laughing; "but I'll risk another
if you will."

"It must only be for a small stake—a single
sesterce," said the infatuated youth, quaffing a
goblet of wine. "I have given up gambling."

"All right," said his friend, "it's only for
amusement that I play," and he cast again, and
laughing paid over his forfeit.

Isidorus continued to win, each time taking
a sip of the strong heady wine. The baleful
enchantment was upon him.

"Double the stakes!" he cried.

"I thought you would tire of our playing like
slaves with jackstones," replied the cool-headed
Calphurnius. "This is something like play," he
continued, as they doubled every time, till the
stakes were soon enormous. The tide of fortune
now turned; but the Greek had become per-
fectly reckless. Conscience was dead, a demon

greed for gain had taken possession of his soul, the gaming-madness surged through his brain. He doubled and redoubled his stakes, till before he rose he had lost even the gold received from Valeria the night before, and was beggared to his last denarius. With blood-shot eyes and staggering gait he reeled away from the table, his handsome features convulsed with rage and wicked imprecations pouring from his lips.

"Don't be so vexed about it, man," said his tormentor, for so he regarded Calphurnius. "Better luck to-morrow. Here I'll lend you enough to set you up. Let us have a bath, we both of us need it to quiet our nerves."

Isidorus, in his maudlin intoxication, accepted the offer, and declared, with much idle babble, that there was more money where that which he had lost came from—that his services were too valuable to the state to be overlooked—and that he knew a thing or two—that he could tell some secrets, if he would—and much more to the same purpose.

This was just what Calphurnius wanted. He had been set on by his father, the Prefect Naso, to worm from the Greek the secrets of the Palace and the Catacomb, and this by a series of wheedling questions he completely succeeded in doing. With some difficulty he got his victim home after he had extorted from him all that he cared to know. When Isidorus awoke next morning it was with feelings of intense disgust with himself and with all the world. He felt that he had played the fool, but how far he knew not. He remembered that he had lost all his money, yet he found a few coins in his purse. He felt that he had forfeited the confidence of his new patron Adauctus, of the Empress, and even was undeserving of the gratitude or respect of the beautiful freed-woman, Callirhoë, whose father he had restored. He had learned that there was a plot on foot against them all. Indeed he had an impression that he had somehow added to their peril by his indiscreet revelations. He determined to warn them of their danger and try to save them.

CHAPTER XVII.

"IN PERICULIS TUTUS."

WITH this purpose the young Greek assuming his most decorous and sober attire, proceeded to what would now be called the bureau of the Chancellor of the Exchequer. It was situated near the Forum, in the cloister around which were grouped the shops of the *argentarii* and *mensarii,* or private and public bankers of Rome. It held about the same relation to those that the Treasury Department at New York does to the bankers' offices and Gold Board in Wall Street. On every side were evidences of the concentrated wealth and power of the august mistress of the world. A vast granite building, as strong and solid as a prison, was before him. Roman sentinels paced the street, hugging the wall to share the protection from the noontide heat offered by its grateful shade. Convoys of specie, guarded by cohorts

of soldiers with unsheathed swords, were con-
tinually arriving or departing. Gangs of sturdy
porters, naked to the waist, were conveying the
heavy iron-bound coffers to and from the vaults.
Officers were counting the tallies and checking
the vouchers, giving and accepting receipts.
Publicans and tax farmers of many hues and
varied garbs were there from many distant climes
—the swart Egyptian, the olive Syrian, the
graceful Greek, the pale-faced yellow-haired
German or Briton. But most prominent of all,
everywhere was seen the pushing, aggressive,
keen-eyed, hook-nosed Jew, who in every age
and every land seems to have had a genius for
finance, banking, and the handling of money.

From the hundred provinces of Rome the
tribute money wrung from wretched peasants,
to support Imperial luxury, to maintain the con-
quering legions, to pay for the largess of corn
that fed the Roman plebs, and for the *fêtes* of
the circus that amused them, and to carry on
the vast governmental administration of the Empire—all poured into this greatest focus of
moneyed wealth in the world. Like Daniel in
Babylon, Adauctus, the Christian, was set over
all this treasure, " because an excellent spirit was
in him, forasmuch as he was faithful, neither
was there any error or fault found in him."
The Emperors, when amid prevailing corruption,

extortion, and fraud, they found an honest servant
and able administrator, winked pretty hard at
his private opinions, so long as they did not
conflict with his duty to the State.   Hence,
from the days of St. Paul, we find that enrolled
among the fellowship of Christ's Church were
" they of Cæsar's household;" and among the
epitaphs of the Catacombs we find frequent
examples of Christians of lofty rank, and holding
important offices of trust; as for instance : "Secretary of the Patrician Order," " Sergeant of the
Exchequer," " Prefect of the City," " Ex-Quæstor
of the Sacred Palace," "Master of the Imperial
Household," and the like.

Making his way to the private apartment, or
office of Adauctus, the Greek found him dictating
despatches to a secretary.   At a nod from his
chief, the secretary retired, and Adauctus, with
warm interest, addressed Isidorus in the words :

"Right welcome, after your successful quest.
You have skilfully performed a difficult task.
The Empress is greatly gratified, and you may
count your fortune as good as made."

"Your Excellency is too kind," replied the
Greek, with a graceful salutation ; "I feel that
I do not deserve your praise."

"Your modesty, my friend," remarked Adauctus
with a smile, "shall not prevent your promotion.
It is too rare a gift not to be encouraged."

"I have come, your Excellency," said Isidorus, with some degree of trepidation, "upon a business that nearly concerns yourself, and some to whom you wish well."

"It is very good of you," Adauctus calmly replied, "but I do not think you can give me any information that I do not already possess."

"I am in duty bound," continued the Greek, "to reveal to your Excellency, what is a secret which is sedulously kept from your knowledge. You have enemies who have vowed your destruction—the Princess Fausta, Furca, the archpriest of Cybele, and the Prefect Naso. They menace also the Empresses Prisca and Valeria, and others in high places suspected of Christianity."

"Is that all you can tell me?" asked Adauctus, with a smile. "Look you," and unlocking an ivory cabinet, he took out a wax-covered tablet on which were inscribed the names of several other conspirators against his life, with the particulars of their plots.

"I have not sought one of these disclosures," he went on, "yet they have come to me from trustworthy sources; sometimes from men whc are themselves Pagan, yet with honest souls that recoil from treachery and murder."

"And you know all this and remain thus calm!" exclaimed the Greek in amazement

"With such a sword of Damocles hanging over *my* head, I am sure I could neither eat nor sleep."

"Have you never read the words," asked Adauctus solemnly, "'The very hairs of your head are all numbered?' and not a sparrow shall fall without your Father's notice. Have you never read of righteous Daniel whom his enemies cast into the lions' den, and how God shut the lions' mouths that they did him no harm. You have seen the pictured story in the Catacombs. So will my God deliver me from the mouth of the lion," and a look of heroic faith transfigured his face—"or," he whispered lower, but with an expression of even more utter trust, "or give a greater victory and take me to Himself."

"Such stoical philosophy, my master," said the Greek with bated breath, "neither Zeno nor Seneca ever taught."

"Nay," said the noble Roman, "it is not stoicism, it is faith. Not in the Porch or Academy is this holy teaching learned, but in the school of Jesus Christ."

"Oh, wretched coward that I am!" cried the Greek, with an impassioned aspiration after a moral courage which he felt almost beyond his comprehension, "would that I had such faith."

"Seek it, my brother," said Adauctus solemnly, "where alone it may be found, at the Cross of

Christ. Whoso apprehends in his soul the meaning of the Great Sacrifice, will thenceforth count not his life dear unto him for the testimony of Jesus."

"But is the way of the Cross such a thorny, bloodstained path?" asked the Greek, with quavering voice. "Are those noble souls, the highborn and beautiful Valeria, the good and gentle Callirhoë, exposed to such appalling perils?"

"We live in troublous times," answered Adauctus. "Christ came not to send peace on the earth but a sword. Whoso will save his life by cowardice and treachery shall basely lose it. Whoso will lose it for Christ's sake shall gloriously and forever find it!"

These words burned into the heart and brain of the craven Greek, and he winced and shrank beneath them as if a hot iron were searing his quivering flesh.

"But we must hope for the best," went on Adauctus more cheerfully. "We must take every precaution. Life and liberty are glorious gifts. We may not rashly imperil them. I trust that our august mistress, standing so near the throne, stands in no peculiar peril; and you may be sure her power will be used for the protection of her friends. So," he added with a laugh of keen intelligence, "if thou hast any special interest in the fair Callirhoë, be sure she enjoys the most potent patronage in Rome."

"But you, take you no precaution for yourself?" entreated the Greek. " You know not the bitterness of the jealousy and hate of your enemies."

" Oh, yes, I do," the Imperial treasurer calmly replied. " As for me, my work is here. By ruling righteously and dealing justly I can prevent much fraud, and wrong, and suffering. I can shield the innocent and frustrate the villany of public thieves—and there are many such in the high places of this degenerate city. Our heroic ancestors decreed that we must never dispair of our country. But I confess, were it not for that salt of Christian faith that preserves the old Roman world, I believe it would sink into moral putrescence. It is this divine leaven which alone can leaven the whole mass."

CHAPTER XVIII

THE MIDNIGHT PLOT.

THE scene of our story is now transferred to the Palace of the Emperor Galerius, one of the most sumptuous of the group of marble buildings which crowned the Palatine Hill. It is the hour of midnight; and in one of the most private chambers of the palace a secret conspiracy is in progress, which has for its object the destruction of the Christians—especially of those high in rank and influence. The lamps in the *aula* and vestibule burned dimly, and, in iron sockets along the outside of the palace walls, flared and smoked torches made of tow covered with a coating of clay or plaster.*

---

* Such torch-holders may still be seen on the walls of the Palazzo Strozzi and in Florence and elsewhere. Torches of the sort we have described were purchased by the writer at Pozzuoli, near Naples.

Fausta, the mother of Galerius, and Furca, the high-priest of Cybele, were already conferring upon their secret plot. With them was Black Juba, who had just returned from gathering, at "the witching hour of night," upon the unhallowed ground set apart for the burning of the dead, certain baleful plants—wolf's bane, bitter briony, and aconite—which she used in wicked spells and incantations. In her native Nubia she had an evil reputation as a sorceress, and in Rome she still carried on by stealth her nefarious art. It was hinted, indeed, in the palace, that by her subtle, deadly potions she fulfilled her own prophecies of ill against the objects of the hatred of her employers.

"'Tis certain," hissed through her teeth the spiteful old Fausta, while murder gleamed from her sloe-black eyes, "that Galerius will not include in the Imperial rescript that painted doll, Valeria. She exerts unbounded fascination over him. It must be the spell of her false religion."

"The spell of her beauty and grace, rather," answered Furca, with a grin.

"What! Are you duped by her wiles, too?" asked Fausta, with bitterness.

"No; I hate her all the more," said the priest; "but I cannot close my eyes to what every one sees."

"It is something that I, at least, do not see,"

muttered the withered crone, whose own harsh features seemed the very incarnation of hatred and cruelty. " If we cannot get rid of her under the decree," she went on, " we can, at least, in a surer but more perilous way. Cunning Juba, here, has access to her person; and by her skilled decoctions can make her beauty waste, and her life flicker to extinction, like a lamp unreplenished with oil."

" Yes, Juba has learned, in the old land of the Nile, some of the dark secrets of Egypt," whispered, with bated breath, the dusky African. " But it is very perilous to use them. The palace is full of suspicion; and that new favourite, Callirhoë,—how I hate her!—keeps watch over her mistress like the wild gazelle of the desert over its mate. It will take much gold to pay for the risk."

" Gold thou shalt have to thy heart's content, if thou do but rid me of that cockatrice, who has usurped my place in my son's affections," hissed the wicked woman, who still felt a fierce, tiger-like love for the soldier-son whom she had trained up like a tiger cub. And Juba retired, to await further orders.

" But if she die thus," said Furca, with a malignant gleam in his eyes, " she dies alone. What we want is to have her drag others down with her—her mother, Prisca; that haughty

Adauctus, who holds himself so high, and the rest of the accursed Christian brood."

"Yes, that is what we want, if it can be done," said Fausta; "but I fear it is impossible. You do not know how headstrong Galerius is in his own way; and the more he is opposed, the fiercer he is."

"Here comes Naso," said the arch priest. "He hates the Christians, if he does not love the gods. We will hear his counsel."

"Welcome, good Naso," exclaimed Fausta, as the Prefect of the city was ushered into the room. "We need your advice in the matter of this edict against the Christians: how we may use it as a net to snare the higher game of the palace and the Imperial household."

"We must be wary as the weasel, sleepless as the basilisk, deadly as the aspic," said Naso, sententiously.

"Just what I have been saying," remarked Furca.

"Methinks we must employ the aspic's secret sting, rather than the public edict."

"I declare for the edict," exclaimed with energy the truculent Naso. "Let its thunders smite the loftiest as well as the lowly. It will carry greater terror, and make the ruin of the Christian party more complete. What is the use of lopping off the twigs, when the trunk and

10

main branches are unscathed? I possess proof that will doom Adauctus, the senator Aurelius, and others who stand higher still. The Christians to the lions—every one, say I."

"And so say I," ejaculated Furca, with malicious fervour; "but her Excellency thinks that Galerius will interpose to protect one who stands near the throne, though she be the chief encouragement of the Christian vermin that crawl at her feet."

"Madam, he dare not," exclaimed Naso, with his characteristic gesture of clenching his hand as if grasping his sword. "His own crown would stand in peril if beneath its shadow he would protect traitors to the State and enemies of the gods, however high their station."

"As head of the State," interjected the priest, "he is the champion of the gods, and bound to avenge their insulted majesty."

"You know not what he would dare," replied Fausta. "He would defy both gods and men, if he took the whim."

"An accusation will be made before me," said Naso, "which not even the Emperors can overlook, against the Imperial Consort, Valeria, for intriguing with the Christians and bringing their priests to Rome, and conniving at their crimes against the State. We will see whether the majesty of the Empire or the beauty of a painted butterfly weighs the heavier in the scales."

"I will second in private what your accusation demands in public," said the implacable Fausta. "Methinks I could die content if I might only trample that minion under my feet."

"And I," said Furca, "will menace him with the wrath of the gods if he refuse to avenge their wrongs."

"Between us all," added Naso, "it will go hard if we do not crush the Christian vermin, even beneath the shadow of the throne."

CHAPTER XIX.

IN THE TOILS OF THE TEMPTER.

IN his statement as to the accusation of the Empress before his tribunal, Naso, after his manner, took counsel of his truculent desires rather than of his cool reason. He had learned from his scapegrace son, Calphurnius, that Isidorus had returned to town from executing a commission for the Empress, the general purpose of which that hopeful youth had extorted from the drunken maunderings of the inconstant and unhappy Greek. Naso took it for granted, from his previous acquaintance with human nature of the baser sort, that Isidorus was trying to serve two masters, and that while acting as the agent of Valeria he would be willing to betray her secrets. Unaware of his vacillation of character and of his transient impulses toward Christianity, he further believed that the supple Greek, in accordance with his compact, would act as public

accuser of the Christians. He had impressed
upon Calphurnius, who was very prompt to learn
the lesson, that it was of the utmost importance
to bring the Greek under his personal influence
and control, and especially to induce him to
come again to the tribunal of the Prefect in the
Forum.

"We must keep our thumb on him. We can
use him to our advantage," said the Prefect to his
son.

"I think I have him under a screw that will
extort from him whatever you wish," replied the
hopeful youth. "He owes me money, and he
shall pay good interest on the loan. He is not
the material of which heroes are made, like that
young Christian who suffered martyrdom, as they
call it, a few weeks ago."

"Well, give your screw another turn," said
Naso with a hideous chuckle. "That's the way
I do when I have them on the rack. Keep him
in debt. Lure him on. Make him lose money
at dice and lend him more. We will wring his
heart-strings by-and-bye. If we can only secure
the death of Adauctus and some of his wealthy
friends, their fair estates will help to line our
purses, for the Emperors cannot leave such a
zealous servant as the Prefect Naso unrewarded,"
and this well matched pair—the offspring of the

corruption and cruelty of the Empire—parted,
each intent on his purposes of evil.

The young scapegrace, Calphurnius—young in
years, but old in vice—followed only too success-
fully this Satanic advice. He attached himself
closely to Isidorus and became his very shadow
—his other self. He lured him on to ostentatious
extravagance of expenditure, often allowing him
to win large sums at dice to replenish his depleted
purse, and again winning from him every sesterce,
and binding the Greek's fortunes more firmly to
his own by lending him large sums, yet demand-
ing usurious interest. The easy, pleasure-loving
nature of Isidorus, intent on enjoying the passing
hour and shrinking from suffering of body or
anxiety of mind, made this *descensus Averni* all
the more facile. He was thus led to forget all
his good resolutions and noble purposes, and to
plunge into the fashionable follies of the most
corrupt society in the world. From the maunder-
ing remarks which fell from his lips in his fits of
drunkenness, for he rapidly lapsed into this bane-
ful vice, Calphurnius constructed a monstrous
story of treachery which he used to create an
utter rupture between the Greek and the Christians, alleging that he had too irreparably betrayed them to be ever forgiven, and that the
only way of escaping the doom which menaced
them was to throw himself into the arms of the

party in power. It was with feelings of horror that in his rare moments of sober reflection Isidorus realized how fast and how far he had drifted from the thoughts, and feelings, and purposes of the hour when he knelt, in the Catacomb of Callixtus, at the feet of the good presbyter Primitius; or since he returned from Milan the restorer to the fair Calirrhoë of her sire; or even since, a few days before, he had conversed with Adauctus and beheld with admiration his serenity of spirit under the shadow of persecution and death.

Calphurnius exhausted every art to wring from his lips a legal accusation of the Christians, for even the ruthless persecutors wished to observe some forms of law in the destruction of their destined victims.

"You have already betrayed them beyond reparation," he said, "and you may as well obtain the reward. You have told all about your employment by Adauctus in a treasonable mission to the Christian sectaries at Ravenna and Milan. You have been present at their assemblies at the Villa Marcella and in the Catacombs. A short hand notary* has taken down every word you said, and it shall be used

* These tachugraphoi were in common employment in the courts, and the sermons of Chrysostom were also reported by their skill.

against you unless you turn evidence for the State, and save yourself by bringing its enemies to justice."

"Wretch!" cried the exasperated Greek. "Cease to torment me! 'Tis you who have tempted me to this perfidy, and now you seek to goad me to perdition. The Christians are no traitors to the State, and you know it."

"The edict of the Emperors declares that they are," said Calphurnius, with a sneer, "perhaps you can persuade their Divine Majesties that they are mistaken."

"What would you? What further infamy would you have me commit?" exclaimed the tortured Isidorus.

"Only declare before the Prefect what you have already divulged to me. By refusing you only imperil yourself," replied his tormentor.

"I consent," moaned the craven-hearted Greek, and he went on with a shudder, "I am double-dyed in infamy already. I can acquire no deeper stain."

"'Tut, man! don't be a fool! Rome can pay her servants well. You will soon be well rewarded," and like an incarnate Diabolus, the accuser of the brethren proceeded to earn, as another Judas, the wages of iniquity by betraying innocent blood.

CHAPTER XX.

THE PLOT THICKENS.

ISIDORUS reluctantly accompanied Calphurnius to the tribunal of the Prefect; and there, partly through intimidation, partly through cajolery, he gave such information as to his expedition to Ravenna and Milan as the Prefect chose to ask. This was tortured, by that unscrupulous officer, into an accusation against the Empress Valeria of conspiracy with the Chancellor, Adauctus, and others of the Christian sect, against the worship of the gods of Rome, and so, constructively, of treason against the State. This indictment—*accusatio*, as it was technically called—was duly formulated, and attested under the seal of the Prefect's Court. Naso, the Prefect, and Furca, the priest, found a congenial task in submitting the document to the Emperor Galerius, and asking his authority to proceed against the accused. They visited the

palace at an hour when it had been arranged
that the Emperor's evil genius, the cruel Fausta,
should be with him, to exert her malign influence
in procuring the downfall of the object of her
malice—the Empress Valeria—and the destruction of the Christian sect. "The insulted gods
appeal to your Divine Majesty for protection,
and for the punishment of the atheists who de-
spise their worship and defy their power," began
the high-priest of Cybele, seeking to work upon
the superstition of the Illyrian herdsman, raised
to the Imperial purple.

"Well, my worthy friend," replied the Emperor
in a bantering tone, "what is the matter now.
Has any one been poaching on your preserves?"

"This is not a matter of private concern, Your
Majesty," remarked the Prefect gravely. "It
touches the welfare of the State and the stability
of your throne."

"Yes, and your personal and domestic honour,
too," whispered Fausta in his ear.

"It must be something pretty comprehensive
to do all that. Come, out with it at once," laughed
the Emperor.

Thus adjured, Furca began to recount the in-
sults offered to the gods by the Christians, and,
especially, that the Empress no longer attended
their public festivals.

"Oh yes, I understand," said the Emperor, with

a yawn, "your craft is in danger. The offerings at your altars are falling off; and we all know where *they* went. The gods are all alike to me; I believe in none of them."

"But they are necessary, to keep the mob in subjection," said Naso. "Some are amused with their pageants, and others are awed by menaces of their wrath."

"Yes, I grant you, they are of some use for that; and that is all they are good for," replied this ancient Agnostic.

"But the Christians are traitors to the State," continued the Prefect; "rank sedition-mongers. They are secretly sworn to serve another Lord than the Cæsars, and they are ceaselessly striving to undermine your Imperial Majesty's authority."

"You do well," continued the cruel Galerius, a fire of deadly hate burning in his eyes, "to exterminate that accursed vermin, wherever found. Burn, crucify, torture, as you will."

"And the estates of the rebels, they escheat to the temples of the insulted gods?" asked the priest, with hungry eyes.

"Nay, to the State, I think," laughed the Emperor. "Is it not so, good Naso?"

"Half to the State and half to the *delator*, or accuser," answered that worthy, learned in the law of pillage.

"Let not the wolves fall out about the prey,"

said the Emperor, with a sneer; "only make sure work."

"Be so good then, Your Majesty, as to affix your seal to these decrees of death. With such high officers as Adauctus and Aurelius my authority as Prefect is not sufficient."

"And the Empress Valeria; she, too, as traitor to your person and crown, is included in the decree," insinuated, in a wheedling tone, the crafty priest.

"Base hound," roared the Emperor, laying his hand upon his sword; "breathe but the name of the Empress again, and I will pluck thy vile tongue from thy throat."

"Nay, Your Majesty," said the crafty Fausta, while the abject priest cowered like a whipped cur; "'tis but his excess of zeal for Your Majesty's honour, which I fear the Empress betrays."

"Madam," said Galerius, sternly, "I am the guardian of my own honour. What the Christians are, I neither know nor care. What the Empress is, I know—the noblest soul that breathes in Rome. Who wags his tongue against her shall be given to the crows and kites. *Dixi. Fiat*—I have spoken—so let it be," and his terrible frown, as he stalked from the room, showed that he meant what he said.

The three conspirators, for a moment, stared at

each other in consternation. Then the wily Fausta faltered out, "Said I not, he would defy both gods and men ? We must do by, stealth what we cannot do by force. Juba must ply her most secret and most deadly arts. I have certain subtle spells myself; and if mortal hate can give them power, I will make her beauty waste away like a fading flower, and her strength wane like a dying lamp."

"'Tis a dangerous game," replied Naso. "Be wary how you play it. As for me, armed with this edict, I will strike at mine ancient foe, for whom I long have nursed a bitter spite. Curse him ! I am tired of hearing him called Adauctus the Just. He held me to such a strict account that I had to make a full return of all the fines and mulcts paid in, without taking the toll which is my right." And he departed to gratify his double passion of revenge and greed.

It may seem strange that such a truculent monster as Galerius, of whom, in his later days, his Christian subjects were wont to say that " he never supped without human blood—*Nec unquam sine cruore humano cœnabat*" *—should be so under the spell of his Christian wife. But the statement is corroborated by the records of history, and by the philosophy of the human mind

* Lactantius, *De Mortibus Persecutorum.*

There is a power in moral goodness that can awe
the rudest natures, a winsome spell that can sub-
due the hardest hearts.   It was the story of Una
and the Lion, of Beauty and the Beast over again;
and one of the severest trials for a Christian
wife in those days of the struggle between Christianity and Paganism for the mastery of the
world, was that of being allied to a pagan husband.   Tertullian, in the third century, thus de-
scribes the difficulties which a Christian woman
married to an idolater must encounter in her
religious life :

"At the time for worship the husband will
appoint the use of the bath; when a fast is to be
observed he will invite company to a feast.
When she would bestow alms, both safe and
cellar are closed against her.   What heathen will
suffer his wife to attend the nightly meetings of
the Church, the slandered Supper of the Lord, to
visit the sick even in the poorest hovels, to kiss
the martyrs' chains in prison, to rise in the night
for prayer, to show hospitality to stranger
brethren ? "*

In time of persecution, or in the case of persons of such exalted rank as that of Valeria, the
difficulty of adorning a Christian life, amid their
pagan surroundings, was all the greater.   Yet not

---

* Tertull, *Ad Uxorem*, ii. 8.

a word of scandal has been breathed upon the
character of the wife of the arch persecutor of
the Christians; and even the sneering pen of
Gibbon has only words of commendation for the
Christian Empress who herself under subsequent
persecution, remained steadfast even unto death.

The beauty and dignity of Christian wedlock
in an age of persecution and strife are nobly
expressed by Tertullian in the following passage,
addressed to his own wife: "How can I paint the
happiness," he exclaims, "of a marriage which
the Church ratifies, the Sacrament confirms, the
benediction seals, angels announce, and our
heavenly Father declares valid! What a union
of two believers—one hope, one vow, one discipline, one worship! They are brother and sister,
two fellow-servants, one spirit and one flesh.
They pray together, fast together, exhort and
support one another. They go together to the
house of God, and to the table of the Lord.
They share each other's trials, persecutions, and
joys. Neither avoids, nor hides anything from
the othe.. They delight to visit the sick, succour
the needy, and daily to lay their offerings before
the altar without scruple, and without constraint.
They do not need to keep the sign of the cross
hidden, nor to express secretly their Christian
joy, nor to receive by stealth the eucharist. They

join in psalms and hymns, and strive who best
can praise God.   Christ rejoices at the sight, and
sends His peace upon them.   Where two are in
His name He also is; and where He is, there evil
cannot come." *

CHAPTER XXI.

A CRIME PREVENTED.

THE deadly malice of Fausta, Furca, and Naso towards the Empress Valeria, foiled in its attempt to invoke upon her the penalties of the edict against the Christians, sought, by secret means, to procure her death. Juba, the black slave, was heavily bribed to prepare some of her most subtle poisons and procure their administration. But here a difficulty presented itself, and it is a striking illustration of the corruption of the Empire and of the daily peril in which the inhabitants of the Imperial palace dwelt—a state of peril which finds its modern analogue only in the continual menace under which the Czar of all the Russias lives, with a sword of Damocles suspended by a single hair above his head. Such was the atmosphere of suspicion which pervaded the whole palace, such the dread of assassination or of poisoning, that trusty guards and

11

officers swarmed in the ante-chambers and prevented access to the members of the Imperial
family except under the most rigid precautions
of safety; and a special officer was appointed,
whose duty, as his title of *Prægustator* implies,
was to taste every kind of food or drink provided for the Imperial table. Regard for his
personal safety was, of course, a guarantee that
the utmost precautions were observed in preparing
the daily food of the Imperial household. Juba
in vain attempted to bribe some of the kitchen
scullions and cooks to mix with the savoury
viands designed for the use of Valeria, who generally lunched in her private apartments, a potent
poison. They accepted, indeed, her bribes, but
prudently declined to carry out their part of the
agreement, well knowing that she dare not ven-
ture to criminate herself by an open rupture with
them.

At length she resolved on attempting a more
subtle but less certain mode of administering a
deadly drug. While in the service of a priest of
Isis in Egypt, she had extorted or cajoled from
an Abyssinian slave in his service certain dark
secrets, learned it was said by the Queen of Sheba
from Solomon, and handed down from age to age
as the esoteric lore of the realm. One of these
was the preparation of a volatile poison so subtle
and powerful that its mere inhalation was of

deadly potency. As a means of conveying this
to her victim, and at the same time of disguising
the pungent aromatic odour, a basket of flowers
which she had plentifully sprinkled with the
deadly poison was sent to the Empress.   To make
assurance doubly sure, she concealed among the
flowers one of those beautiful but deadly asps,
such as that from the bite of which the dusky
Queen of Egypt, the wanton Cleopatra, died.
This, for purposes connected with her nefarious
arts, she had procured—as what evil thing could
not be procured?—from the dealers in deadly
drugs, philtres, and potions in the crowded Ghetto
of Rome.

To ensure the conveyance of the deadly gift
to the hands of Valeria herself, Juba invented
the fiction that they were a thankoffering from
the young Greek, Isidorus, to his Imperial pa-
troness for favours received. With her characteristic cunning Juba had possessed herself of
the secret of his services rendered to the Empress,
and of the interest felt in him by her august
mistress.

Valeria was in her *boudoir* with her favourite
and now inseparable Callirhoë, as her tire woman,
dressing her hair, when the fatal missive arrived.
As Callirhoë received the basket from the hands
of Juba, the eyes of the slave gleamed with the
deadly hate of a basilisk, and she muttered as she
turned away—

"May the curse of Isis rest on them both. My fine lady has driven black Juba from the tiring room of the Empress. May she now share her fate," and, like a sable Atropos, she glided from the chamber with stealthy and cat-like tread.

"Oh! what fresh and fragrant flowers," exclaimed the Empress Valeria, as she bent over them, "see how the dew is yet fresh upon their petals." Here she raised the basket so as more fully to inhale their fragrance. At that moment the concealed and deadly asp whose dark green and glossy skin had prevented its detection among the acanthus and lily leaves, siezed, with his envenomed fang, the damask cheek of the fair Valeria, and for a moment clung firmly there.

"O God, save her!" exclaimed Callirhoë, who in a moment recognized the cruel aspic, of which, as a child, she had been often warned in her native Antioch, and with an eager gesture she flung the venomous reptile to the ground and crushed its head beneath her sandal's heel. On the quick instinct of the moment and without stopping to think of the consequences to herself, she threw her arms about her Imperial mistress' neck, and pressing her lips to her cheek, sucked the venom from the yet bleeding wound.

The cry of the Empress as the little serpent stung her cheek brought a swarm of attendants and slaves into the room, among them black Juba

and the officer of the guard who was responsible
for the Empress' safety. Valeria had fainted and
lay pale as ashes on her couch, a crimson stream
flowing from her cheek.

"Dear heart!" exclaimed Juba, with an ostentatious exhibition of well-feigned grief, "let her
inhale this fragrant elixir. It is a potent restora-
tive in such deadly faints," and she attempted to
complete her desperate crime by thrusting the
poisonous perfume under Valeria's nostrils.

"Who was last in the presence before this
strange accident—if it be an accident—occurred?"
demanded the officer.

"I and Juba, were the only ones," faltered
Callirhoë, when a deathly pallor passed over her
face, and with a convulsive shudder she fell writhing on the ground.

"You are under arrest," said the officer to
Juba, and then to a soldier of the guard, "Go,
seize and seal up her effects—everything she has;
and you," turning to another, "send at once the
court physician."

The attendants meanwhile were fanning and
sprinkling with water the seemingly inanimate
forms of the Empress and Callirhoë. When the
physician came and felt the fluttering pulse and
noted the dilated eyes of his patients, he pronounced it a case of acrid poisoning and promptly
ordered antidotes. The Empress, in a few days

rallied and seemed little the worse beyond a strange pallor which overspread her features and an abnormal coldness, almost as of death, which pervaded her frame. From these she never fully recovered, but throughout her life was known in popular speech as " The White Lady."

Upon Callirhoë the effects of the poison were still more serious. By her prompt action in sucking the aspic virus from the envenomed wound, she had saved the life of her beloved mistress, but at the peril of her own. The venom coursed through her veins, kindling the fires of fever in her blood. Her dilated eyes shone with unusual brilliance ; her speech was rapid ; her manner urgent ; and her emotions and expressions were characterized by a strange and unwonted intenseness. The physician in answer to the eager questioning of Valeria, gravely shook his head, and said that the case was one that baffled his skill—that cure there was none for the aspic's poison if absorbed into the system, although as it had not in this case been communicated directly to the blood, possibly the youth and vigour of the patient might overcome the toxic effect of the contagium—so he learnedly discoursed.

" My dear child, you have given your life for mine," exclaimed the Empress, throwing her arms around her late enfranchised slave, and bedewing her cheek with her tears.

"God grant it be so," said Callirhoë, with kindling eye. "I would gladly die to save you from a sorrow or a pain. I owe you more than life. I owe you liberty and a life more precious than my own."

"All that love and skill can do, dear heart, shall be done," said the Empress caressingly, "to preserve you to your new-found liberty, and to your sire."

"As God wills, dearest lady," answered Callirhoë, kissing her mistress' hand. "In His great love I live or die content. I bless Him every hour that He has permitted me to show in some weak way, the love I bear my best and dearest earthly friend."

And with such fond converse passed the hours of Valeria's convalescence, and of Callirhoë's deepening decline.

CHAPTER XXII.

THE STORM BURSTS.

THE crafty Juba, when she found herself arrested in *flagrante delicto*—in the very act of her attempted crime—determined to use, if possible, the fiction she had employed with reference to Isidorus, as a means of escape from the very serious dilemma in which she was placed. It will be remembered that she had stated, in order to procure the acceptance of her fatal gift, that it was a thank-offering from the young Greek who had rendered such service to the Empress and Callirhoë. Happy if Valeria had remembered and practised the ancient adage, " *Timeo Danaos et dona ferentes.*" But suspicion was foreign to her generous nature, and even if the wise saw had occurred to her, she would have lightly laughed away its cynical suggestion.

When the treacherous slave was examined as to her share in the attempted crime, she stoutly adhered to her fictitious story, and protested that she knew nothing of the contents of the basket, but that she had received it from Isidorus, and had been well paid for conveying it to the Empress without suspicion of any sinister design.

The Greek, when charged with the crime of attempting to procure, by poison, the death of the Empress Valeria, manifested the greatest astonishment. Summoned before the Quæstor of the Palace, an officer of co-ordinate jurisdiction with the Prefect of the city, he stoutly protested his innocence. But all his protestations were regarded by that official, as only the very perfection of art—the well-feigned evasions of a mendacious Greek. And certainly appearances were very much against him. The Prefect Naso, now that he had extorted from him all the information he had to give, abandoned him as a worn-out tool and divulged to the Quæstor the damning fact that the Greek by a formal document had accused the Empress of treason against the State, and of conspiracy with the Christians—for so he represented the confessions which, by his diabolical arts, he had wrung from his unhappy victim. Confronted by this evidence Isidorus was dumb. He saw the trap into which he had been snared, and that by no efforts of his own could he extricate himself. He saw, too, the ruin he had brought upon his friends, for Naso had procured the immediate arrest of Adauctus, Aurelius, and Demetrius, the father of Callirhoë, and other Christians connected with the Imperial household. Callirhoë herself was also placed under arrest, upon the monstrous accusation of conspiracy with Isidorus and Juba to procure the death of the Empress Valeria. One would have thought that her self-devotion and almost sacrifice of her life to save that of her mistress would have been a sufficient vindication from such a charge. But the unreasoning terror of the Emperors and the unreasoning hatred of all who bore the Christian name, fostered as these were by the machinations and evil suggestions of the Quæstor of the Palace, the Prefect of the city, the arch priest of Cybele, and the cruel, crafty Fausta, thirsty for the blood of her victim, rendered possible the acceptance of any charge, however improbable. "Any stick will do to beat a dog," and any accusation, however absurd, was considered available against the Christians.

Even Galerius who, left to himself, would, soldier-like, have braved any personal danger, completely lost his judgment at the peril menacing the Empress. The tortures of slaves and servants by the perverted tribunals, miscalled of justice, fomented by the cruel, crafty priests, and the eager greed of Prefect and Quæstor, caused an outburst of persecution against all who bore the Christian name. The estates of Adauctus, and Aurelius were expropriated by the persecutors, and as a consequence their late possessors were pre-judged to death. Valeria who would fain have interposed her protection, had suffered such a physical shock as to be incapable of exercising any authority or influence she might possess. And the Empress Prisca, less courageous in spirit, less beautiful in person, and less potent in influence, was completely cowed by the domineering violence of the Emperor Diocletian, who was quite beside himself at the conspiracy against the gods, and against the Imperial Household which he persuaded himself had been discovered.

"Madam," he replied, in answer to a weak remonstrance against the persecution, "was it not enough that our palace at Nicomedia was burned over our heads, that you must apologise for treason in our very household and the menace of our very person. No; the Christian superstition must be stamped out, and the worship of the gods maintained." *

Hence throughout the wide empire, in the sober language of history, "Edict followed edict, rising in regular gradations of angry barbarity. The whole clergy were declared enemies of the State; and bishops, presbyters, and deacons were crowded

* These are the very words of the edict quoted in note to Chapter II.

into the prisons intended for the basest malefactors "*—"an innumerable company," says the
Christian bishop Eusebius, "so that there was
no room left for those condemned for crime."
"We saw with our own eyes," writes a contemporary historian, "our houses of worship thrown
down, the sacred Scriptures committed to the
flames, and the shepherds of the people become
the sport of their enemies—scourge with rods,
tormented with the rack and excruciating
scrapings, in which some endured the most terrible death. Then men and women, with a
certain divine and inexpressible alacrity rushed
into the fire. The persecutors, constantly inventing new tortures, vied with one another as if
there were prizes offered to him who should
invent the greatest cruelties. The men bore fire,
sword, and crucifixions, savage beasts, and the
depths of the sea, the maiming of limbs and
searing with red hot iron, digging out of the eyes
and mutilations of the whole body, also hunger,
the mines, and prison. The women also were
strengthened by the Divine Word, so that some
of them endured the same trials as the men, and
bore away the same prize. It would exceed all
powers of detail," he goes on, "to give an idea
of the sufferings and tortures which the martyrs
endured. And these things were done, not for

* Milman, History of Christianity, Book II., Chapter ix.

a few days, but for a series of whole years. We ourselves," he adds, " have seen crowds of persons, some beheaded, some burned alive, in a single day, so that the murderous weapons were blunted and broken in pieces, and the executioners, weary with slaughter, were obliged to give over the work of blood."* And he goes on to describe deeds of shame and torture of which he was an eye-witness, which our pen refuses to record.

The enthusiasm for martyrdom prevailed at times almost like an epidemic. It was one of the most remarkable features of the ages of persecution. Notwithstanding the terrific tortures to which they were exposed, the zeal of the Christian heroes burned higher and brighter in the fiercest tempest of heathen rage. Age after age summoned the soldiers of the Cross to the conflict whose highest guerdon was death. They bound persecution as a wreath about their brows, and exulted in the "glorious infamy" of suffering for their Lord. The brand of shame became the badge of highest honour. Besides the joys of heaven they won imperishable fame on earth; and the memory of a humble slave was often haloed with a glory surpassing that of a Curtius or Horatius. The meanest hind was ennobled by the accolade of martyrdom to the

* Eusebius' " Ecclesiastical History," Book VIII., Chaps. ii-xiv.

loftiest peerage of the skies. His consecration of suffering was elevated to a sacrament, and called the baptism of fire or of blood.

Burning to obtain the prize, the impetuous candidates for death often pressed with eager haste to seize the palm of victory and the martyr's crown. ᐧThey trod with joy the fiery path to glory, and went as gladly to the stake as to a marriage feast. "Their fetters," says Euse-bius, "seemed like the golden ornaments of a bride."* They desired martyrdom more ardently than men afterward sought a bishopric.† They exulted amid their keenest pangs that they were counted worthy to suffer for their divine Master. "Let the ungulæ tear us," exclaims Tertullian;‡ "the crosses bear our weight, the flames envelope us, the sword divide our throats, the wild beasts spring upon us; the very posture of prayer is a preparation for every punishment." "These things," says St. Basil, "so far from being a terror, are rather a pleasure and a recreation to us."∥

* Hist. Eccles., v. 1.

† Multique avidius tum martyria gloriosis mortibus quærebantur quam nunc episcopatus pravis ambitionibus appetuntur.—Sulpic. Sever. Hist., lib. II.

‡ Apol. c. 30.

∥ Gregory Nazianzen. Orat. de Laud. Basil. See also the striking language of Ignatius. Euseb. Hist. Eccles. iii. 36.

"The tyrants were armed," says St. Chrysostom; "and the martyrs naked; yet they that were naked got the victory, and they that carried arms were vanquished."* Strong in the assurance of immortality, they bade defiance to the sword.

Though weak in body they seemed clothed with vicarious strength, and confident that though "counted as sheep for the slaughter," naught could separate them from the love of Christ. Wrapped in their fiery vesture and shroud of flame, they yet exulted in their glorious victory. While the leaden hail fell on the mangled frame, and the eyes filmed with the shadows of death, the spirit was enbraved by the beatific vision of the opening heaven, and above the roar of the mob fell sweetly on the inner sense the assurance of eternal life. "No group, indeed, of Oceanides was there to console the Christian Prometheus; yet to his upturned eye countless angels were visible—their anthem swept solemnly to his ear —and the odours of an opening paradise filled the air. Though the dull ear of sense heard nothing, he could listen to the invisible Coryphæus as he invited him to heaven and promised him an eternal crown."† The names of the "great army

* Chrys. Hom. 74, de Martyr.

† Kip, p. 88—from Maitland, p. 146. Sometimes the ardour for martyrdom rose into a passion. Eusebius says (Hist. Eccles., viii., 6) that in Nicomedia "Men

of martyrs," though forgotten by men, are written
in the Book of Life. " The Lord knoweth them
that are His."

> There is a record, traced on high,
> That shall endure eternally ;
> The angel standing by God's throne
> Treasures there each word and groan ;
> And not the martyr's speech alone,
> But every wound is there depicted,
> With every circumstance of pain—
> The crimson stream, the gash inflicted—
> And not a drop is shed in vain.*

This spirit of martyrdom was a new principle
in society. It had no classical counterpart.†
Socrates and Seneca suffered with fortitude, but
not with faith. The loftiest pagan philosophy
dwindled into insignificance before the sublimity
of Christian hope. This looked beyond the
shadows of time and the sordid cares of earth

and women with a certain divine and inexpressible
alacrity rushed into the fire."

* Inscripta.CHRISTO pagina immortalis est,
 Excepit adstans angelus coram Deo.
 Et quæ locutus martyr, et quæ pertulit :
 Nec verbum solum disserentis condidit,
 Omnis notata est sanguinis dimensio,
 Quæ vis doloris, quive segmenti modus :
 Guttam cruoris ille nullam perdidit.—*Peristeph.*

† The pagans called the martyrs βιαθάνατοι, or self
murderers.

to the grandeur of the Infinite and the Eternal. The heroic deaths of the believers exhibited a spiritual power mightier than the primal instincts of nature, the love of wife or child, or even of life itself. Like a solemn voice falling on the dull ear of mankind, these holy examples urged the inquiry, "What shall it profit a man if he gain the whole world and lose his own soul?" And that voice awakened an echo in full many a heart. The martyrs made more converts by their deaths than in their lives. "Kill us, rack us, condemn us, grind us to powder," exclaims the intrepid Christian Apologist; "our numbers increase in proportion as you mow us down."* The earth was drunk with the blood of the saints, but still they multiplied and grew, gloriously illustrating the perennial truth—*Sanguis martyrum semen ecclesiæ.*

* Tertul., Apol., c. 50.

CHAPTER XXIII.

THE MAMERTINE PRISON.

ET us now turn our attention to the fate of the characters in our tale of Christian trial and triumph, around whom its interest chiefly centres. They have been consigned to one of the most dismal of the many gloomy dungeons of Rome —the thrice terrible Mamertine prison—haunted with memories of long centuries of cruelty and crime. Manacled each to a Roman soldier, Adauctus, Aurelius, Demetrius, and Callirhoë, together with other Christians condemned to martyrdom, marched through the streets under the noontide glare of a torrid sun. A guard armed *cap à pié*, flung open an iron-studded door, and admitted them to a gloomy vault a few steps below the level of the street. Here a brawny Vulcan, with anvil and hammer, with many a brutal gibe smote off the fetters that linked the prisoners and soldiers together, and riveted them again so that these victims of oppression were bound together in pairs. Sometimes it happened that one of a pair thus bound together died, and the survivor endured the horror of being inseparably fettered to a festering corpse. To this the apostle refers when, groaning over the corruptions of his sinful nature, he exclaims: "O wretched man that I am, who shall deliver me from the body of this death ?"

"My dainty lady," said the hideous Cyclops, as he rudely seized the arm of Callirhoë, "this is not the sort of bracelet you've been used to wear. I should not much mind being bound to such as you myself, only I would prefer silken fetters to those iron gyves." Then, as she shrank from his touch and winced as he bruised her tender flesh in unriveting the fetters, he said, with an insolent jeer, "I wont hurt you more than I can help, my beauty. You are not used to having such a rough chamberlain;" and he uttered a coarse jest with which we shall not pollute our page.

A rosy flush stormed the brow of the maiden as she turned her blushing cheek to the mildewed and cold stone wall, in haughty silence disdaining a word of reply to the brutal ruffian.

"Nay, my fine gentlemen," went on this typical Roman jailer, as Adauctus and the aged Demetrius, weary with their march, sank upon a stone bench, "this is too luxurious an apartment for you. For you we have a deeper depth." And he pointed to an opening in the floor, hitherto unnoticed in the gloom. "Nay, you need not shrink, old man," he went on, as Demetrius recoiled from the grave-like opening at his feet. "Your betters have been there before you."

"Father, your blessing e'er you go," exclaimed Callirhoë, and flinging herself on his breast, she received his kiss and benediction.

By means of a leathern strap beneath their arms, the prisoners were one by one let down into a hideous vault, like men to a living burial. Into this lower dungeon no beam of light struggled, save a precarious ray from the opening in the floor above. The loathsome cell was even then dank with the slime of well-nigh a thousand years, its construction being attributed to Ancus Martius, the fourth king of Rome. Here the African prince, Jugurtha, was starved to death. "What a cold bath is this!" he exclaimed, as he descended into its chilly gloom. Here the Gallic king, Vercingetorix, also died. Here the usurper Sejanus was executed, and here the fellow conspirators of Cataline lingered to death. If we would accept Roman tradition, we would also believe that St. Peter and St. Paul were immured in this dismal vault, and in the case of the latter illustrious martyr it is more than likely that the

story is true. A stairway has now been constructed to this lower depth, and the present
writer has stood upon the stone pavement worn
by the feet of generations of victims of oppression, and has drunk of a spring at which the
Apostle of the Gentiles may have quenched his
thirst.

The prisoners enjoyed not long even this sad
reprieve from death. They were destined soon
to finish their course by a glorious martyrdon.
The Emperors determined to gratify at once their
own persecuting fury and the cruel thirst for
blood of the Roman mob, by offering a holocaust
of victims in the amphitheatre. The *Acta Diurna*,
a sort of public gazette of the day, which cir-
culated in the great houses, and baths, and other
places of concourse, contained the announcement
of a grand exhibition of the *ludi circenses*, or
gladiatorial games, to be celebrated in honour of
the god Neptune—*Neptunus Equestris*. In the
public spaces of the Forum, and in the neighbour-
hood of the Flavian Amphitheatre and elsewhere,
where the crowd around them would not obstruct
the highway, were displayed large white bulletin
boards, on which were written in coloured chalks
a list of the games—like the playbills which
placard the streets of great cities to-day—and
heralds proclaimed through every street, even in
the crowded Ghetto, the splendour of the ap-

proaching games. These were on a scale oı which
no modern manager ever dreamed. Trajan exhibited games which lasted a hundred and twenty-
three days, in which 10,000 gladiators fought and
11,000 fierce animals were killed. Sometimes
the vast arena was flooded with water, and
naumachia or sea-fights were exhibited. The vast
flood-gates and cisterns by which this was accomplished may still be seen.

The chief attraction of the games provided by
the Emperors Diocletian and Galerius, however,
was not the conflict of what might almost be
called armies of trained gladiators, nor the
slaughter of hundreds of fierce Libyan leopards
and Numidian lions, but the sacrifice of some
scores of helpless and unarmed Christians—old
men, weak women, and tender and innocent
children.

There was much excitement in the schools of
the gladiators—vast stone barracks, where they
were drilled in their dreadful trade. They were
originally captives taken in war, or condemned
malefactors; but in the degenerate days of the
Empire, knights, senators, and soldiers sought
distinction in the arena, and even unsexed women
fought half-naked in the ring, or lay dead and
trampled in the sands. To captives of war was
often offered, as a reward for special skill or
courage, their freedom, and fierce and fell were

conflicts to which men were spurred by the double incentives of life and liberty.

Special interest was given to the forthcoming games by the distinguished reputationof one of the volunteer gladiators, a brilliant young military officer, our friend Ligurius Rufus, who, sated and sickened with the most frenzied dissipations that Rome could offer, plunged into this mimic war to appease by its excitement the gnawing *ennui* of his life.

The bets ran high upon the reckless young noble who was the favourite of the sporting spend-thrifts and profligates of the city. The vilest condition of society that ever cursed the earth was filling up the measure of its iniquity, and invoking the wrath of Heaven. The wine shops in the Suburra and the gladiators' quarter were overflowing with a brawling, blaspheming,drunken mob, the vilest dregs of the vilest city the patient earth has ever borne upon its bosom.

CHAPTER XXIV.

THE EVE OF MARTYRDOM.

FAR different was the scene presented by another spot not far distant—a vaulted chamber beneath the stone seats of the Coliseum, whither the destined Christian martyrs had been removed on the eve before the day of their triumph. As an act of grace, some coarse straw, the refuse of a lion's lair, had been given them, and the relief to their fetter-cramped limbs, stiffened with lying on a rough stone floor, was in itself an indescribable delight. But they had a deeper cause of joy. They were found worthy to witness a good confession for Christ before Cæsar, like the beloved Apostle Paul; and even as their Lord Himself before Pontius Pilate. And now the day of their espousals to their Heavenly Bridegroom was at hand.

The silvery-haired Demetrius, a holy calm beaming in his eyes, uttered words of peace and

comfort. The coarse black barley-bread and muddy
wine which had been given them lest death should
cheat the mob of their promised delight on the
morrow, the venerable priest had consecrated to
the Supper of the Lord—the last viaticum to
strengthen their souls on their journey to the
spirit world. Sitting at his feet, faint and wan,
but with a look of utter content upon her face,
was his daughter Callirhoë, a heavenly smile
flickering about her lips. With an undaunted
courage, a heroic resolve beaming from his eyes,
stood Adauctus, waiting, like a valiant soldier at
his post, the welcome word of the great Captain
of his salvation: "Well done! good and faithful
servant, enter thou into the joy of thy Lord."

Ever and anon the deep-mouthed roar of a
hungry lion rent the air, his fierce bound shook
the walls of his cage, and his hot breath came
through the bars as he keenly sniffed the smell
of human flesh. But though it caused at times
a tremor of the quivering nerves of the wan and
wasted girl, it shook not her unfaltering soul.
Listen to the holy words calmly spoken by the
venerable Demetrius: "'*Non turbetur cor vestrum*
—Let not your heart be troubled. In my Father's
house are many mansions. I go to prepare a
place for you.' Yes, daughter. Yes, brave friend;
before another sun shall set we shall see the King
in His beauty, and the land that is very far off.

Mine aged eyes shall see, too, the beloved Rachel
of my youth, to behold whom they have ached
these many years. And thou, child, shalt see
the mother after whom thy heart hath yearned."

"If only, dear father, my brother Ezra were
with us," whispered Callirhoë, "we soon would
be an unbroken family in the city of the great
King."

"God's will be done, my child," answered the
patriarch. "He doeth all things well. He could
bid His angels fly swiftly, and shut the lions'
mouths, or better still, convoy our spirits to the
marriage supper of the Lamb—to the repose of
Abraham's bosom. Your brother is a child of the
covenant, an heir of the promises, the son of
many prayers. God will count him also in the
day when He maketh up His jewels." Then,
as if gifted with the spirit of prophecy, he
exclaimed: "Not always shall the servants of
the Most High be persecuted unto death. But
this very structure, now dedicated to slaughter
and cruelty, shall hereafter be consecrated to the
service of the true God"—a prediction which,
after long centuries, has been literally fulfilled.

Thus in holy converse wore the hours away.
And then through the rocky vaults of the Coliseum
stole the sweet accents of their last evening
hymn before they should sing the song of Moses
and the Lamb on high :—

"He that dwelleth in the secret place of the Most High, shall abide under the shadow of the Almighty.

"I will say of the Lord, He is my refuge and my fortress, my God, in Him will I trust.

"He shall give His augels charge over thee, to keep thee in all thy ways.

"Thou shalt tread upon the lion and adder; the young lion and the dragon shalt thou trample under foot."

As this pæan of triumph swelled into louder strain, the gladiators, awed by its strange power, paused amid their ribald jests, and even the lion hushed his hungry roar. and the tiger his angry growl.

CHAPTER XXV

A ROMAN HOLIDAY.

EARLY next morning the army of slaves who had charge of the Coliseum, under the direction of Fulvus, the freedman, were hard at work. Some at the very summit of the building, with much shouting and pulling of ropes, were stretching the great *velarium* or awning, as a protection from the rays of the sun. Others were sweeping the sand of the arena to a smooth and even surface. Many cart loads of fresh sand were heaped around the base of the *podium*, for the ghastly purpose of being spread upon the blood-stained surface after each act of the sanguinary drama of the day. Others were decorating with garlands of flowers, and with gold and purple bannerets, the seats of the Emperors Diocletian and Galerius, and those of the senators and other persons of distinction. The great structure seemed even more striking in its vastness, as a few score

figures crawled like flies over its empty seats,
than when filled with its tumultuous throng of
spectators.   It was an immense oval six hundred
and fifteen feet in its longer diameter, and five
hundred and ten feet in the shorter.   The circling
seats rose tier on tier to the giddy height of one
hundred and fifty feet.

As the present writer climbed those cliff-like
walls, now crumbling into ruin, he tried to re-
people those long-deserted seats with the eager
and excited throngs which had often filled them
to overflowing, when twice eighty thousand cruel
eyes were wont to gloat upon the dying martyr's
pang, "butchered to make a Roman holiday."*
Then he wandered through the vast vaulted corridors and stairways, eighty in number, and
bearing still the old Roman numerals by which
access was gained to the different galleries.   These
were so capacious that the whole multitude could
in a few minutes disperse, and were thence called
vomitoria.   He then explored the dens and caves
for the wild beasts, and the rocky chambers in

---

*On this very arena perished the venerable Ignatius,
linked by tradition with the Saviour Himself as one of
the children whom He took in His arms and blessed.
" Suffer me to be the food of wild beasts," he exclaimed,
"by whom I shall attain unto God.   For I am the wheat
of God, and I shall be ground by the teeth of wild
beasts, that I may become the pure bread of Christ."

which the gladiators and martyr victims awaited
the signal that called them to their doom.   The
row of seats just above the *podium* was reserved
for the equestrian order; those higher still, for
the *populus*, or common people; and the highest
of all, for persons of the lowest rank.   Early in
the day, multitudes of spectators began to arrive,
mostly arrayed in gala dress, and many wearing
the colours of their favourite gladiatorial champion.   With a loud flourish of trumpets the great
gates of the imperial entrance opened, and the
chariots of the Emperors and their respective
suites entered and took their places in the grand
tribune reserved for these august occupants.   It
was noted with dissatisfaction by the multitude
that neither of the Empresses Prisca or Valeria,
were present.   But the withered old crone Fausta,
mother of Galerius, seemed to gloat like a foul
harpy on the anticipated spectacle of blood, and
near by was her sinister shadow, the black-browed
priest of Cybele.

   Our old acquaintance, Burdo, the butcher, was
rubicund with joy at the approaching conflict, for
. which, he said, he long had hungered.   "But
why," he asked, "are not their majesties, the
Empresses, in the state tribune.   'Tis a contempt
of a festival sacred to the gods."

   " Our dainty Empress," jeered Samos, the "Flat-
:ose," "has small stomach to see her friends the

Christians given to the lions, and I suspect the old one is tarred with the same stick."

"If I thought that I'd denounce her myself," growled Bruto, the gladiator; "Empress or slave. the crime of being a Christian levels all ranks."

"And lose your head for your pains," chimed in Piso, the barber. "Don't you know that she winds the Emperor round her finger like a silken thread."

"Does she favour the accursed Nazarenes ? " croaked Ephraim the Jew. " May the same fate overtake her."

"I thought they were friends of yours," said our old friend Max, who was one of the soldiers on guard. "They say this Christus whom they worship was a Jew."

We dare not repeat the wicked imprecation which burst from the lips of the exasperated Israelite. But it is notorious that the Jews were far more malignant persecutors of the Christians than even the Pagans themselves—as is apparent from the Acts of the Apostles and other records of the early Church.

The time for beginning the games having come, the priest of Neptune poured a libation to the god, and heaped incense on his altar, placed near the Imperial tribune. In this act of worship— for these old gods were worshipped with the blood of men slain as a holiday pageant—he was fol- lowed by the Emperors and their chief officers.

Then with another peal of trumpets a procession of gladiators in burnished armour entered the arena and marched around its vast circuit. Pausing before the tribune of the Emperors they chanted with a loud voice : " *Cæsares Augusti, morituri salutarus vos*—Great Cæsars, we who are about to die salute you."

First there was a sort of sham battle—*prælusio,* as it was called, in which the gladiators fought with wooden swords. But the multitude were speedily impatient of that, and demanded the combat *a l'outrance*—to the death.

" We came not here to witness such child's play as that," said Burdo, the butcher. " I want to see the blood flow as it does in my own shambles ; " a brutal sentiment which met with much favour from his neighbours.

Soon their desires were gratified. First there was a combat of *Andabatæ,* that is, men who wore helmets without any aperture for the eyes, so that they were obliged to fight blindfold, and thus excited the mirth of the spectators. Although they inflicted some ugly wounds upon each other, none of these were mortal, and the mob called loudly for the *Hoplomachi,* who were next on the play-bill. These were men who fought in a complete suit of armour. They were as completely encased as crabs in their shells, but as they could see each other through the bars of their visors, they were able skilfully to direct their weapons at the joints of their antagonist's armour. Soon the arena was red with blood, and more than one victim lay dead and trampled on the sands.

"Good! this is something like the thing," cried Burdo. "But these fellows are so cased in their shells it is hard to get at them. Let us have the *Retiarii.*"

"Yes, the *Retiarii* and *Mirmillones,*" shouted the mob; and they soon marched upon the scene.

This conflict promised abundance of excitement. The *Retiarii* wore no armour, and their only weapons were a net (*rete*, hence their name) and a trident or three-pronged spear. The *Retiarius* endeavoured to throw the net over his antagonist, and then to despatch him with the spear. If he missed his aim in throwing his net, he betook himself to flight, and endeavoured to prepare his net for a second cast, while his adversary followed him round the arena in order to kill him before he could make a second attempt. It was a cruel sport, and kindled to fury the fierce passions of the eager spectators.

Then came a conflict between skilled gladiators —the most accomplished swordsmen of the gladiatorial school. The vast multitude watched with fevered interest the wary fencing, the skilful guard and rapid thrust and stroke of those trained butchers of their fellow-men. When a swords-

13

man was wounded, the spectators rent the air with cries of " *Habet! Habet!* " and the one who was vanquished lowered his arms in token of submission. His fate, however, depended upon the will of the people, who sometimes, when a vanquished swordsman had exhibited especial dexterity and skill, gave the signal to spare him by stretching out their hands with the thumbs turned down. But if, as was more frequently the case, their bloodthirsty passions were roused to insatiable fury, they demanded his death by turning their thumbs upwards, and shouting, " *Recipe ferrum!* " Without a tremor the victim then bared his breast to the sword, and the victor thrust it home to the hilt, while the cruel mob shouted their huzzas over the bloody tragedy.

Such is the scene brought vividly before our minds by the matchless antique statue of the Dying Gladiator, found in the Gardens of Sallust, now in the museum of the Capitol. As one gazes with a strange fascination on that wondrous marble, instinct, it seems, with mortal agony, callous must be the heart that is unmoved by its touching pathos. The exquisite lines of Byron nobly express the emotions which it awakens in every breast :—

> I see before me the Gladiator lie :
> He leans upon his hand—his manly brow
> Consents to death, but conquers agony,

And his drooped head sinks gradually low—
And through his side the last drops ebbing slow
From the red gash fall heavy, one by one,
Like the first of a thunder shower ; and now
The arena swims around him—he is gone,
Ere ceased the inhuman shout which hailed the
    wretch who won.

He heard it, but he heeded not--his eyes
Were with his heart, and that was far away.
He recked not of the life he lost nor prize,
But where his rude hut by the Danube lay,
There were his young barbarians all at play,
There was their Dacian mother—he, their sire,
Butchered to make a Roman holiday.

An unwonted interest was given to this cruel
scene in the Roman amphitheatre, by a novel and
unheard of incident which occurred. The brilliant young Roman officer, Ligurius Rufus, we
have said, was announced to take part in these
games. It was no uncommon thing for military
fops, eager to win the applause of the multitude,
or to goad their jaded weariness of life into a
momentary excitement by a spice of real danger,
to enter the lists of the arena; and Ligurius was
at once the most brilliant swordsman in the
Twelfth Legion, and the most *ennuyée* and world-
weary man in Rome.

He was pitted against a brawny Hercules, the
strongest and hugest of the whole school of
gladiators—a British prisoner of war, who had

been long the pride and boast of the arena. As they stood face to face, the young officer in burnished armour, inlaid with silver and gold, and the mighty thews of his opponent encased in leather and bronze, the betting was heavy in favour of the British giant. Each felt that he had a foeman worthy of his steel. They walked warily around each other, each watching with eager eye every movement of his antagonist. Every thrust on either side was skilfully parried, any advantage of strength on the part of the British warrior being matched by the superior nimbleness of the Roman officer. At last a rapid thrust by Ligurius severed a tendon in the sword-arm of his foe, and it fell nerveless by his side. With a giant effort the disabled warrior sprang upon the Roman as if to crush him by sheer weight; but Ligurius nimbly sprang aside, and his antagonist, slipping in the gory sand, fell headlong to the ground. In an instant the Roman's foot was on his neck and his sword at his breast. With a courteous gesture, Ligurius raised his sword and waved it toward the Emperors' tribune and to the crowded seats of the *podium*, as if asking the signal to spare the vanquished gladiator, while the despairing look of the latter seemed with mute eloquence to ask for life. "*Habet! Habet!*" rang round the Coliseum, but not a single sign of mercy was made, not a single thumb was reversed. "*Recipe fer-rum,*" roared the mob at the prostrate giant; and then shouted to Ligurius, "*Occide! Occide!*—Kill! Kill!"

The gallant Roman heeded them as he would heed the howl of wolves. "I am not a butcher," he said, with a defiant sneer, and he sheathed his sword and, much to the surprise of his discom-fitted foe, lent his hand to raise him from the ground.

"You are a brave man," he said, "I want you as a standard bearer for the Twelfth Legion. That is better than making worm's meat of you. Rome may need such soldiers before long."

The Emperors were not unwilling to grant this novel request of a favourite officer, and the grateful creature, in token of his fidelity, humbly kissed the hand of Ligurius, and followed him from the arena. The cruel mob, however, angered at being deprived of their anticipated spectacle of blood, howled with rage, and demanded the crowning scene of the day's sports—the conflict between the wild beasts and the Christian martyrs.

These hateful scenes had become the impas-sioned delight of all classes, from the Emperors to the "vile plebs" of Rome. Even woman's pitiful nature forgot its tenderness, and maids and matrons gloated on the cruel spectacle, and the honour was reserved for the Vestal Virgin to give the signal for the mortal stroke. Such scenes created a ferocious thirst for blood throughout society. They overthrew the altar of pity, and impelled to every excess and refinement of barbarity. Even children imitated the cruel sport in their games, schools of gladiators were trained for the work of slaughter, women fought in the arena or lay dead and trampled in the sand.

It is to the eternal praise of Christianity that it suppressed these odious contests, and forever averted the sword of the gladiator from the throat of his victim. The Christian city of Constantinople was never polluted by the atrocious exhibition. A Christian poet eloquently denounced the bloody spectacle. A Christian monk, roused to indignation by the hateful scene, leaped over the barrier to separate the gladiators in the very frenzy of the conflict. The maddened mob, enraged at this interruption of their sport, stoned him to death. But his heroic martydom produced a moral revulsion against the practice, and the laws of Honorius, to use the language of Gibbon, "abolished forever the human sacrifices of the amphitheatre."

It remains to notice in another chapter the last scene in the stern drama of this "Roman holiday."

CHAPTER XXVI.

THE MARTYRS CROWNED.

AT a flourish of trumpets the iron-studded doors of the cells in which the Christians were confined were thrown open, and the destined martyrs walked forth on the arena in the sight of assembled thousands. It was a spectacle to arrest the attention of even the most thoughtless, and to move the sympathy of even the most austere. At the head of the little company walked the good presbyter, Demetrius, his silvery hair and beard and benignant expression of countenance giving him a strikingly venerable aspect. Leaning heavily on his arm, evidently faint in frame but strong in spirit, was his daughter Callirhoë. Robed in white, she looked the embodiment of saintly purity, and in her eyes there beamed a heroic courage which inspired a wonder that so brave a soul should be shrined in so frail a body. Adauctus, Aurelius, and other Christian confessors condemned to death, made up the little contingent of the noble army of martyrs.

The prefect Naso, from his place in the tribune, near the Emperors, read the sentence of the court, that the accused having been proven by ample testimony to be the enemies of the Cæsars and of the gods, had been condemned to death by exposure to wild beasts.

"Nay, not the enemies of the Cæsars," exclaimed the aged Demetrius. "We are the friends of all, the enemies of none.* We pray for the Cæsars at all our assemblies."

"Will you do homage to the gods ?" demanded Diocletian. "Will you burn incense to Neptune ? Here is his altar and here are his priests."

"We worship the true God who made the heavens and the earth, the sea and all that in them is," replied the venerable man, with uplifted and reverent countenance, "and Him only will we serve. They be no gods which are made by man's device, and 'tis idolatry to serve them."

"Away with the Atheists," cried the priests of Neptune; "they blaspheme the holy gods."

"The Christians to the lions !" roared the mob, and at the signal from the Emperor to the master of the games, the dens of the wild beasts were thrown open, and the savage brutes, starved into

*This famous phrase dates from the time of Tertullian, in the 3rd century, and is also recorded in the Catacombs.

madness, bounded into the arena. The defenceless
martyrs fell upon their knees in prayer, and
seemed conscious only of the presence of Him
who stood with the three Hebrews in the fiery
furnace, so rapt was the expression of faith and
courage on their upturned faces.

The fierce Numidian lions, and tigers from the
Libyan desert, instead of bounding upon their
prey, began to circle slowly around them, lashing
their tawny flanks meanwhile, glaring at their
victims from bloodshot fiery eyes, and uttering
horrid growls.

At this moment a loud shout was heard, and a
soldier, clad in burnished mail, and with his
drawn sword in his hand, one of the body guards
of the Emperors, leaped from the tribune and
bounded with clashing armour into the arena.
Striding across the sand, he hurled aside his iron
helmet and his sword, and flung himself at the
feet of the aged priest, with the words :—

" Father, your blessing; Callirhoë, your parting
kiss.   I, too, am a Christian.   Long time have I
sought you, alas! only to find you thus.   But
gladly will I die with you, and, separated in life,
we are united in death and forever."

" *Nunc dimittis, Domine !* " exclaimed the old
man, raising his eyes to heaven.   " ' Now, Lord,
lettest thou thy servant depart in peace.' "   And
he laid his hands in blessing on the head of his
long-lost son.

"Ezra, my brother!" exclaimed Callirhoë, folding him in her arms. "To think we were so near, yet knew not of each other. Thank God, we go to heaven together; and, long divided on earth, we shall soon, with our beloved mother, be a united family forever in the skies. 'And God shall wipe away all tears from our eyes; and there shall be no more death, neither sorrow nor crying, neither shall there be any more pain.'"

"Amen! even so, come, Lord Jesus!" spake the young soldier, as he enfolded, as if in a sheltering embrace, the gray-haired sire and the fair-faced girl.

The utmost consternation was exhibited on the countenance of the old Emperor Diocletian. "What! have we Christians and traitors even in our body guard? Our very life is at the mercy of those wretches!"

"I would feel safer with them," said the more stoical or more courageous Galerius, "than with the *delators* and informers who betray them," and he glanced with mingled contempt and aversion at Naso, the prefect, and Furca, the priest. "When a Christian gives his word, 'tis sacred as all the oaths of Hecate. I want no better soldiers than those of the Thundering Legion."*

* The *Legio Tonans*, tradition affirms, was a legion composed wholly of Christians, whose prayers in a time of drought brought on a violent thunder-storm, which confounded the enemy and saved the army.

Meanwhile the wild beasts, startled for a moment by the sudden apparition of the mail-clad soldier, seemed roused thereby to ten-fold fury. Crouching stealthily for the fatal spring, they bounded upon their prey, and in a moment crashing bones and streaming gore appeased the growing impatience of the cruel mob, who seemed, like the very wild beasts, to hunger and thirst for human flesh and blood.

We dwell not on the painful spectacle. The gallant young soldier was the first to die. The brave girl, with a gesture of maiden modesty, drew her dishevelled robe about her person, and with a queenly dignity awaited the wild beast's fatal spring. She was mercifully spared the spectacle of her father's dying agony. Her overstrung nerves gave way, and she fell in a swoon upon the sands. Demetrius met his fate praying upon his knees. Like Stephen, he gazed steadfastly up into heaven, and the fashion of his countenance was suddenly transfigured as he exclaimed: " Lord Jesus ! Rachel, O my beloved ! we come, we come." And above the roar of the ribald mob and the growl of the savage beasts, fell sweetly on his inner ear the song of the redeemed, and burst upon his sight the beatific vision of the Lord he loved, and for whom he gladly died.

So, too, like brave men, victorious o'er their

latest foe, Adauctus, Aurelius, and the others calmly met their fate. When all the rest were slain, a lordly lion approached the prostrate form of Callirhoë, but she was already dead. She had passed from her swoon, without a pang, to the marriage supper of the Lamb—to the presence of the Celestial Bridegroom—the fairest among ten thousand, the one altogether lovely—to whom the homage of her young heart had been fully given. She was spared, too, the indignity, of being mangled by the lion's jaws. When the king of beasts found that she was already dead, he raised his massy head, gave a mournful howl, and strode haughtily away.

In the great gallery of Doré paintings at London, is one of this Flavian Amphitheatre after a human sacrifice such as we have described. There lie the mangled forms upon the gory and trampled sands. The sated wild beasts prowl listlessly over the arena. The circling seats rise tier above tier, empty and desolate. But poised in air, with outspread wings, above the slain, with a countenance of light and a palm of victory, is a majestic angel; and sweeping upward in serried ranks, amid the shining stars, is a cloud of bright-winged angels, the convoy of the martyrs' spirits to the skies. So, doubtless, God sent a cohort of sworded seraphim to bear the martyrs of our story blessed company, and to sweep with them through the gates into the city.

CHAPTER XXVII.

THE MARTYRS BURIED.

ARKER and darker grew the shadows of night over the great empty and desolate amphitheatre, but a few hours before clamorous with the shouts and din of the tumultuous mob. The silence seemed preternatural, and a solemn awfulness seemed to invest the shrouded forms which lay upon the sand. By a merciful provision of the Roman law, it made not war upon the dead, and the bodies even of criminals were given up to their friends, if they had any, that they might not be deprived of funeral rites. Having wreaked his cruel rage upon the living body, the pagan magistrate at least did not deny the privilege of burial to the martyrs' mutilated remains. It was esteemed by the primitive believers as much an honour as a duty, to ensepulchre with Christian rites the remains of the sacred dead.*

* See Eusebius, Hist. Eccl., vii., 16 and 22. Eutychianus, a Roman Christian, is recorded to have buried three hundred and forty-two martyrs with his own hands.

Faustus, the faithful freedman of Adauctus, Hilarus, the fossor, and the servants of the Christian matron, Marcella, came at the fall of night to bear away the bodies of the martyrs to their final resting-place in the silent Catacomb. The service was not devoid of danger, for vile informers prowled around seeking to discover and betray whomsoever would pay the rites of sepulture to the remains of the Christian martyrs. But there are golden keys which will unlock any doors and seal any lips, and Marcella spared not her wealth in this sacred service.

On the present occasion, too, special facility was given for carrying out this pious purpose. Through the influence of the Empress Valeria, Hilarus, the fossor, was enabled to show to the chief custodian of the amphitheatre an authorization under the hand of Galerius for removing the bodies of the " criminals who had paid the penalty of the law "—so ran the rescript.

Beneath the cliff-like shadow of the Coliseum gathered this little Christian company. The iron gates opened their ponderous jaws. By the fitful flare of a torch weirdly lighting up the vaulted arches, with gentle and reverent hands, as though the cold clay could still feel their lightest touch, the bodies of the dead were laid upon the biers. Through the silent streets, devout men in silence bore the martyrs to their burial. Through the

Porta Capena, which opened to the magic spell of the Emperor's order; through the silent "Street of Tombs," still lined with the monuments of Rome's mighty dead, wended slowly the solemn procession. There was no wailing of the pagan *nœnia* or funeral dirge, neither was there the chanting of the Christian hymn. But in silence, or with only whispered utterance, they reached the door of the private grounds of the Villa Marcella.

First the bodies were borne to the villa, where, by loving hands, the stains of dust and blood were washed away. Then, robed in white and bestrewn with flowers, they were placed on the biers in the marble atriun. Again the good presbyter Primitius read the words of life as at the burial of Lucius, the martyr,* and vows and prayers were offered up to God.

While this solemn service was in progress, a lady, deeply-veiled, was seen to be agitated by violent grief. Convulsive sobs shook her frame, and her tears fell fast. When the forms of the martyrs were uncovered, that their friends might take their last farewell, the Empress Valeria, for it was she, flung herself on her knees beside the body of the late slave maiden, and rained ears of deep emotion on her face. More lovely in death than in life, the fine-cut features seemed

* See Chapter VI.

like the most exquisite work of the sculptor
carved in translucent alabaster.   A crown of
asphodel blossoms—the emblems of immortality
—encircled her brow, and a palm branch—the
symbol of the martyr's victory—was placed upon
her breast.

"Give her an honoured place among the holy
dead," said the Empress, amid her sobs, to the
venerable Primitius.

"I have given orders," said the Lady Marcella,
"that she, with her father and brother, shall sleep .
side by side in the chamber prepared as the last
resting-place for my own family.   We shall count
it a precious privilege, in God's own good time,
to be laid to rest near the dust of His holy confessors and martyrs."

"Aurelius shall share the tomb," said Hilarus,
the fossor, "which he made for himself while yet
alive, beside his noble wife, Aurelia Theudosia.

"Be it mine to honour with a memorial tablet
the remains of my good master Adauctus," said
Faustus, the freedman, with deep emotion.*

---

* Through the long lapse of ages this memorial has
been preserved, and may still be read in Gruter's great
collection of ancient inscriptions.   It is also referred to
in Gibbon.   In the epitaph occur the following fine lines:

INTEMERATA FIDE CONTEMPTO PRINCIPE MVNDI
CONFESSVS XRM CAELESTIA REGNA PETISTI.

"It shall be my privilege," said the Empress, "to provide for my beloved handmaiden, as a mark of the great love I bore her, a memorial of her saintly virtues; and let her bear my name in death as in life, so that those who read her epitaph may know she was the freedwoman and friend of an unhappy Empress."

The Empress Valeria now retired, and with her trusty escort, returned to the city.

With psalms and hymns, and the solemn chanting of such versicles as: "*Convertere anima mea, in requiem tuam*"—"Return unto thy rest, O my soul;" and "*Si ambulavero in medio umbræ mortis, non timebo mala*"—"Though I walk through the valley of the shadow of death, I shall fear no evil," the funeral procession wound its way, by gleaming torchlight, through the cypress glades of the garden to the entrance of the Catacomb of Callixtus. Here additional torches and tapers were lighted, and carefully the sacred burdens were carried down the long and narrow stair, and through the intricate passages to the family vault of the Lady Marcella.

This vault was one of unusual size and loftiness, and had been especially prepared for holding religious service during the outbreak of perse-

"With unfaltering faith, despising the lord of the world, having confessed Christ, thou dost seek the celestial realms."

14

cution. Marcella held the office of deaconess in the Christian Church, and when even the privacy of her own house was not a sufficient safeguard against the prying of pagan spies, she was wont

SUBTERRANEAN ORATORY, CATACOMB OF CALLIXTUS.

to retire to the deeper seclusion of this subterranean place of prayer. On each side of the door were seats hewn in the solid rock, one for the deaconess, the other for the female catechist who shared her pious labours. Around the wall was a low stone seat for the female catechumens, for the most part members of her own household, who here received religious instruction.   The accompanying engraving indicates the appearance of this ancient oratory or class-room, its main features unchanged, although the lapse of centuries has somewhat marred its structure and defaced its beauty.

With solemn rites and prayers the remains of the martyrs were consigned to their last long resting-place.   Amid the sobs and tears of the mourners, the good presbyter Primitius paid a loving tribute to their holy lives and heroic death —all the more thrilling because they themselves stood in jeopardy every hour.   In the presence of the martyred dead the venerable pastor then broke the bread and poured the wine of the Last Supper of the Lord, and the little company of worshippers seemed united in still closer fellowship with those who now kept the sacred feast in the kingdom of their common Father and God.

Before they left the chamber, Hilarus, after he had hermetically sealed the tombs of Demetrius and Ezra, his son, cemented with plaster a marble slab against the opening of that on which was laid—rude couch for form so fair—the body of the chief subject of our " ower true tale."   As it was designed to be but a temporary memorial of the virgin martyr, until the costly epitaph which the Empress was to provide should be ready, he took the little pot of pigment which he had

brought for the purpose, and 'th his brush in,
scribed the brief sentence :—

VALERIA DORMIT IN PACE.

ANIMA DULCIS, INNOCVA, SAPIENS ET PVLCHP   IN
XRO.

QVI VIXIT ANNOS XVIII.   EN. V. DIES X.

"Valeria sleeps in peace. A sweet spirit—guileless, wise, beautiful—in Christ. She lived
eighteen years, five months, ten days."

"VALERIA SLEEPS IN PEACE."

Alas! the time never came when that costly
memorial should be reared. The violence of
persecution soon drove the Empress herself an
exile from her home, and when the storm rolled
away there was none left to carry out her pious
wish. Through the long centuries that humble
epitaph was all the memorial of one of the noblest,
sweetest, bravest souls that ever lived. And even
that rude slab was not destined always to cover

her remains. After the re-discovery of the Catacombs in the sixteenth century, many of their
tombs were pillaged for relics, or in the vain
search for treasure. By some ruthless rifler of
the grave this very slab was shivered, and the
lower part of the epitaph destroyed; and there
upon its rocky bed, on which it had reposed for
well-nigh fifteen hundred years, lay in mouldering
dust the remains of the maiden martyr, Valeria
Callirhoë.   Verily *Pulvis et umbra sumus!*

Primitius and Hilarus, with the little company
of devout men who bore the martyrs to their
burial, now proceeded to the entombment, in a
neighbouring crypt, of the bodies of Adauctus
and Aurelius. As they advanced through the
dark corridors, but dimly lighted by their tapers'
feeble rays, the silence of that under-world
seemed almost appalling. Black shadows crouched
around, and their footsteps echoed strangely down
the distant passages, dying gradually away in this
vast valley of the shadow of death. Almost in
silence their sacred task was completed, and they
softly sang a funeral hymn before they turned to
leave their martyred brethren to their last long
sleep.

Suddenly there was heard the tumultuous
" tramp, tramp," as of armed men. Then the clang
of iron mail and bronze cuirass resounded through
the vaulted corridors. The glare of torches was

seen at the end of a long arched passage, and the sharp, swift word of military command rang out stern and clear.

"Forward! Seize the caitiffs! Let not one escape! Slay if they resist!" and a rush was made to the chamber where the notes of the Christian psalm had but now died away.

"Out with your lights!" exclaimed, in a muffled tone, Hilarus, the fossor. "Follow me as closely and as quietly as you can. Good Father Primitius, your arm. By God's help we will disappoint those hunters of men of their anticipated prey."

"Or join our brethren in martyrdom, as is His will," devoutly added Primitius. "He doeth all things well."

But we must go back a little to learn the cause and means of this armed invasion of the Catacombs.

CHAPTER XXVIII.

THE BETRAYAL—THE PURSUIT.

WHEN the unhappy Isidorus discovered that through his cowardice and tergiversation, and through the confessions extorted from his distempered mind, a criminal charge had been trumped up against the fair Callirhoë, whose beauty and grace had touched his susceptible imagination, he was almost beside himself with rage and remorse. He protested to the Prefect Naso and his disreputable son, Calphurnius, that she was as innocent as an unweaned babe of the monstrous crime alleged against her—that of conspiracy to poison her beloved mistress.

"Accursed be the day," cried the wretched Isidorus, clenching his hands till his nails pierced the flesh, " accursed be the day when I first came to your horrid den to betray innocent blood. Would I had perished e'er it dawned."

"Hark you, my friend," said Naso, " do you

remember by what means you promised to earn the good red gold with which I bought you ? "

" Do not remind me of my shame in becoming a spy upon the Christians," cried the Greek with a look of self-loathing and abhorrence.

" Nay ; 'by becoming one yourself,' that was the phrase as I wrote it on my tablets," sneered the prefect.

" Would that I could become one ! " exclaimed the unhappy man.

" Suppose I take you at your word and believe you are one ? " queried Naso with a malignant leer.

" What new wickedness is this you have in your mind?" asked the Greek.

" How would you like to share the doom of your friends, the old Jew and his pretty daughter, who are to be thrown to the lions to-day," went on the remorseless man, toying with his victim like a tiger with its prey.

" Gladly, were I but worthy," said the Greek. " Had I their holy hopes, I would rejoice to bear them company."

" But don't you see," said Naso, " a word of mine would send you to the arena, whether you like it or not ? Your neck is in the noose, my handsome youth, and I do not think, with all your dexterity, you can wriggle out of it."

"Oh! any fate but that!" cried the Greek, writhing in anguish. "Let me die as a felon, a conspirator, an assassin, if you will; but not by the doom of the martyrs."

"Well, you see," went on the prefect, "justice is meted out to the Christians so much more swiftly and certainly than even against the worst of felons, that I am tempted to take this plan to secure you your deserts."

The craven-spirited Greek, to whom the very idea of death was torture, blanched with terror and stood speechless, his tongue literally cleaving to the roof of his mouth.

When the prefect perceived that he was sufficiently unnerved for his final experiment he unveiled his diabolical purpose.

"Hark you, my friend," he whispered or rather hissed into his ear, "you may do the State, yourself, and me a service, that will procure you life and liberty and fortune. You know the way to the secret assemblies of the accursed Christian sect; lead hither a maniple of soldiers and your fortune's made."

"Tempter, begone!" exclaimed the Greek in a moment of virtuous indignation, "you would make me worse than Judas whom the Christians execrate as the betrayer of his Master whom they worship."

"As you please, my dainty youth," answered Naso, with his characteristic gesture of clutching his sword. "Prepare to feed the lions on the morrow," and he consigned him to a cell in the vaults of the Coliseum.   •

Very different was the night spent by this craven soul to that of the destined martyrs. The darkness, to his distempered imagination, seemed full of accusing eyes, which glared reproach and vengeance upon him. The hungry lions' roar smote his soul with fearful apprehensions. When the savage ,bounds of the wild beasts shook his cell he cowered upon the ground, the picture of abject misery and despair.

When by these mental tortures his nerves were all unstrung, the arch tempter silently entered his cell and whispered in his ear, "Well, my dainty Greek, are you ready for the games?"

"Save me! save me!" cried the unhappy man, "any death but that! I will do anything to escape such a fearful doom."

"I thought you would come to terms," replied the prefect, well skilled in the cruel arts of his office. "Life is sweet. Here is gold. By the service I require you shall earn liberty," and the compact was sealed whereby the Greek was to betray the subterranean hiding-places of the Christians to their enemies.

Hence it was that at the dead of night, a band of Roman soldiers, reckless ruffians trained to slaughter in many a bloody war, marched under cover of darkness along the Appian Way to the villa of the Lady Marcella. It was the work of a moment to force the door of the vineyard and they soon reached the entrance to the Catacomb.

"It is like a badger's burrow," said the officer in command. "We will soon bag our game. Here the old priest has his lair. Secure him at any cost. He is worth a score of the meaner vermin."

Lighting their torches they marched on their devious way under the guidance of Isidorus, who had written on a rude chart the number of turns to be made to the right or left. With Roman military foresight, the officer marked with chalk the route they took, and fixed occasionally a torch in the niches in the wall.

Soon the soft, low cadence of the funeral hymn was heard, stealing weirdly on the ear, and a faint light glimmered from the chamber in which the Christians were paying the last rites to their martyred brethren.

"They are at their incantations now," said the Centurion. "'Tis a fit place for their abominable orgies. Let us hasten, and we will spoil their wicked spells!" and he gave the command, at which the soldiers rushed forward toward the distant light.

Instantly it disappeared, and when they reached the spot naught was seen, save the tomb of Adauctus; and in the distant darkness was heard the sound of hurrying feet.

" The rats have fled," cried the officer; " after them, ferrets! Let not one escape !" and at the head of the maniple he darted down the echoing corridor.

But Hilarus guided his friends amid the darkness more swiftly than the soldiers could pursue by the light of their torches. He followed many a devious winding, especially contrived to frustrate capture, and facilitate escape. Threading a very narrow passage, he drew from a niche a wooden ladder, and placing it against the wall reached a stairway which began high up near the roof. The whole party followed, and Hilarus, drawing up the ladder after him, completely cut off pursuit. They soon reached the comparatively lofty vaults of a deserted *arenarium,* or sand pit, which communicated with the open air. As he stood with bared brow beneath the light of the silent stars, the good Presbyter Primitius devoutly exclaimed: —"*Anima nostra sicut passer erepta est de laqueo venantium*—Our soul is escaped as a bird out the snare of the fowler, the snare is broken and we are escaped."

The writer has not drawn upon his imagination in describing the arrangements for escape made by the persecuted Christians, when taking refuge in these dens and caves of the earth. In this very Catacomb of Calixtus, such a secret stairway still exists, and is illustrated by drawings in his book on this subject. The main entrance was completely obstructed, and the stairway partially destroyed, so as to prevent ingress to the Catacomb, and a narrow stairway was constructed in the roof which could only be reached by a moveable ladder, connecting it with the floor. By drawing up this ladder pursuit could be easily cut off, and escape to a neighbouring *arenarium* secured. Stores of corn, and oil, and wine have been found in these crypts, evidently as a provision in time of persecution ; frequent wells also occur, amply sufficient for the supply of water ; and the multitude of lamps which have been found would dispel the darkness, while their sudden extinction would prove the best concealment from attack by their enemies. Hence the Christians were stigmatized as a skulking, darkness-loving race,* who fled the light of day to burrow like moles in the earth. These labyrinths were admirably adapted for eluding

* Latebrosa et lucifugax natio.—*Minuc. Felix.*

pursuit. Familiar with their intricacies, and following a well-known clew, the Christian could plunge fearlessly into the darkness, where his pursuer would soon be inextricably lost.

Such hairbreadth escapes as we have described from the Roman soldiers, like sleuth hounds tracking their prey, must have been no uncommon events in those troublous times. But sometimes the Christians were surprised at their devotions, and their refuge became their sepulchre. Such was the tragic fate of Stephen, slain even while ministering at the altar; such the event described by Gregory of Tours, when a hecatomb of victims were immolated at once by heathen hate; such the peril which wrung from a stricken heart the cry, not of anger but of grief, recorded on a slab in the Catacombs: *Tempora infausta, quibus inter sacra et vota ne in cavernis quidem salvari possimus!*—"Oh! sad times in which, among sacred rites and prayers, even in caverns, we are not safe." It requires no great effort of imagination to conceive of the dangers and escapes which must have been frequent episodes in the heroic lives of the early soldiers of the cross.

With what emotions must the primitive believers, seeking refuge in these crypts, have held their solemn worship and heard the words of life, surrounded by the dead in Christ! With what power would come the promise of the resurrection cf the body, amid the crumbling relics of mortality! How fervent their prayers for their companions in tribulation, when they themselves stood in jeopardy every hour! Their holy ambition was to witness a good confession even unto death. They burned to emulate the zeal of the martyrs of the faith, the plumeless heroes of a nobler chivalry than that of arms, the Christian athletes who won in the bloody conflicts of the arena, or amid the fiery tortures of the stake, not a crown of laurel or of bay, but a crown of life, starry and unwithering, that can never pass away. Their humble graves are grander monuments than the trophied tombs of Rome's proud conquerors upon the Appian Way. Reverently may we mention their names. Lightly may we tread beside their ashes·

Though the bodily presence of those conscripts of the tomb no longer walked among men, their intrepid spirit animated the heart of each member of that little community of persecuted Christians, ' of whom the world was not worthy; who wandered in deserts, and in mountains, and in dens and caves of the earth, . . being destitute, afflicted, tormented."*

---

* Compare the following spirited lines of Bernis :—
" La terre avait gemi sous le fer des tyrans ;
Elle cachait encore des martyrs expirans,
Qui dans les noirs detours des grottes reculees
Derobaient aux bourreaux leurs tetes mutilees."
Poeme de la Religion Vengee, chap viii.

CHAPTER XXIX.

THE DOOM OF THE TRAITOR.

BUT what, meantime, had become of the pursuers? Baffled in their effort to seize their prey, and fearful of losing their way in this tangled labyrinth they had sullenly retreated, tracing their steps by the chalk-marks they had made upon the walls. At last, they returned to the stairway by which they had entered and so found their way above ground.

"This is no work for soldiers," muttered the disgusted officer, "hunting these rats through their underground runs. They are a skulking set of vermin."

"What has become of that coward Greek?" asked the second in command. "He didn't seem to half like the job."

"Is he not here? Then he must have made his escape," said the Centurion. "But if he is caught in that rat-trap, there let him stay. I'll not risk a Roman soldier's life to save a craven Greek," and he gave the command to march back to the city.

Meanwhile, how fares it with the unhappy Isidorus?

When the soldiers caught sight of the Christians and began their pursuit, he had no heart to join in it, and lingered in the vaulted chamber where the funeral rites had been interrupted. The first thing that caught his eye was the epitaph of the noble Adauctus. With quavering voice he read the lines we have already given: "With unfaltering faith, despising the lord of the world, having confessed Christ, thou dids't seek the celestial realms."

"And this was he," he soliloquised, "who gave up name, and fame, and fortune, high office, and the favour of the Emperor, and embraced shame, and persecution, and a cruel death for conscience sake. How grand he was that day when I warned him of the machinations of his foes—so undaunted and calm. But grander he is as he lies in the majesty of death behind that slab. I felt myself a coward in his living presence then, but in the presence of this dead man, I feel a greater coward still. His memory haunts, it tortures me, I must away!" and turning from the chamber he wandered by the dim light of his taper down the grave-lined corridor, pausing at times to read their humble inscriptions :—

Rudely written, but each letter
Full of hope, and yet of heart-break,
Full of all the tender pathos
Of the here and the hereafter.

And their calmness and peacefulness seemed to reproach his conscience-smitten and unrestful soul.

Listlessly he turned into another chamber, when, what was it that met his startled vision !—

VALERIA DORMIT IN PACE.

There slept in the sleep of death another victim of his perfidy, one whom he had longed to save, one whose beauty had fascinated his imagination, whose goodness had touched his heart. Overcome by his emotion he flung himself on the ground, and bursting into convulsive sobs that shook his frame, he passionately kissed the cold stone slab on which was written the much-loved name.

" Would that I, too, slept the sleep of death," he exclaimed; " if I might also sleep in peace; if I might seek celestial realms. . . So near and yet so far . . A great gulf fixed . . Never to see thee more . . in time nor in eternity."

Here the drip, drip of water which had infiltrated through the roof and fell upon the floor,

jarred upon his excited nerves, and suddenly, with
a hissing splash, fell a great drop on his taper and
utterly extinguished its light. For a moment,
so intense and sudden was the darkness, he was
almost dazed; but instantly the greatness of his
peril flashed upon his mind.   •

" Lost! Lost!" he frantically shrieked. "The
outer darkness, the eternal wailing—while she is
in the light of life! Well I remember now the
words of Primitius, in this very vault, as he spoke
of the joys of heaven, the pains of hell;" and in
the darkness he tried to trace with his finger the
words, " DORMIT IN PACE "—"Sleeps in peace."

" *Vale! Vale! Eternum Vale!*" he sobbed, as
he kissed once more the marble slab, " an everlasting farewell!   I must try to find the Christians, or the soldiers, or a way of escape from this
prison-house of graves."

He groped his way to the door of the vault and
listened, oh! so eagerly—all the faculties of his
body and mind seeming concentered in his sense
of hearing. But "the darkness gave no token and
the silence was unbroken." Nay, so awful was
the stillness that brooded over this valley of death,
that it seemed as if the motion of the earth on
its axis must be audible, and the pulses of his
temples were to his tortured ear like the roaring
of the distant sea.

Venturing forth, he groped his way from grave

to grave, from vault to vault, from corridor to corridor, but no light, no sound, no hope! Ever denser seemed the darkness, ever deeper the silence, ever more appalling the gloom. For hours he wandered on and on till, faint with hunger, parched with thirst, the throbbings, of his heart shaking his unnerved frame, he fell into a merciful swoon from which he never awoke. Centuries after, an explorer of this vast necropolis found crouching in the corner of one of its chambers a' fleshless skeleton, and on the tomb above he read the words, VALERIA DORMIT IN PACE. Was it accident or Providence, or some strange instinct of locality that had brought this poor blighted wreck to breathe his latest sigh at the tomb of one whom he had so loved and so wronged?

The peasants of the Campagna tell to the present day of certain strange sounds heard at midnight from those hollow vaults—at times like the hooting of an owl, at times like the wailing of the wind, and at times, they whisper with bated breath, like the moaning of a soul in pain. And the guides to the Catacombs aver, that ever on the anniversary of the martyrdom of Valeria Callirhoë, sighs and groans echo through the hollow vaults—the sighs and groans, tradition whispers, of a wretched apostate who in the ages of persecution betrayed the early Christians to a martyr's doom.

CHAPTER XXX.

FATE OF THE PERSECUTORS--TRIUMPH OF CHRISTIANITY.

IT remains only to trace briefly the fate of the unfortunate Empress Valeria—less happy than her lowly namesake, the martyr of the Catacombs—and the doom of the persecuting tyrants. In the violent and bloody deaths, often more terrible than those which they inflicted on the Christians, which overtook, with scarce an exception, these enemies of the Church of God, the early believers recognized a divine retribution no less inexorable than the avenging Nemesis of the Pagan mythology.*

Diocletian, smitten by a mental malady, abandoned the throne of the world for the solitude of his palace on the Illyrian shores of the Adriatic,

* See Lactantius, *De Mortibus Persecutorum, Passim*; Eusebius *Hist. Ecclec.* viii. 17 ; ix. 9, 10 ; Tertullian *ad Scap.*, c. 3.

where tradition avers that he died by his own hand.

A still more dreadful doom befell the fierce persecutor, Galerius. Consumed by the same loathsome and incurable disease which is recorded to have smitten his great rivals in bloodshed, Herod the Great and Philip II., from his dying couch he implored the prayers of the Christians, and, stung by remorse for his cruelties, commanded the surcease of their long and bitter persecution.

The Empress Valeria, his widow, by her beauty had the ill fortune to attract the regards of his successor in persecution, the Emperor Maximin. Spurning his suit with the scorn becoming a pure and high-souled woman, at once the daughter and widow of an Emperor, she encountered his deadly hate. Her estates were confiscated, her trusted servants tortured, and her dearest friends put to death.

"The Empress herself," says Gibbon, "together with her mother, Prisca, was condemned to exile ; and as they were ignominiously hurried from place to place, before they were confined to a sequestered village in the deserts of Syria, they exposed their shame and distress to the provinces of the East, which during thirty years, had respected their august dignity." On the death of

Maximin, Valeria escaped from exile and repaired in disguise to the court of his successor, Licinius, hoping for more humane treatment. But these hopes, to use again the language of Gibbon, "were soon succeeded by horror and astonishment, and the bloody execution which stained the palace of Nicomedia sufficiently convinced her that the throne of Maximin was filled by a tyrant more inhuman than himself. Valeria consulted her safety by hasty flight, and, still accompanied by her mother Prisca, they wandered above fifteen months through the provinces in the disguise of plebeian habits. They were at length discovered at Thessalonica; and as the sentence of their death was already pronounced, they were immediately beheaded and their bodies thrown into the sea. The people gazed on the melancholy spectacle; but their grief and indignation were suppressed by the terrors of a military guard. Such was the unworthy fate of the wife and daughter of Diocletian. We lament their misfortunes, we cannot discover their crimes." *

At length, on the triumph of the British-born Emperor, Constantine, over his rivals for the throne of the world, like the trump of Jubilee,

---

* Valeria quoque per varias provincias quindecim mensibus plebeio cultu pervagata. . . . Ita illis pudicitia et conditio exitio fuit. Lactantius *De Mort. Persec.* Cap. 51.

the edict of the toleration of Christianity, pealed through the land. It penetrated the gloomy dungeon, the darksome mine, the Catacombs' dim labyrinth, and from their sombre depths, vast processions of "noble wrestlers for religion," thronged to the long-forsaken churches, with grateful songs of praise to God.

Christianity, after long repression, became at length triumphant. It emerged from the conceal-ment of the Catacombs to the sunshine of imperial favour. Constantine, himself, proclaimed to eager thousands the New Evangel—the most august lay preacher the Church has ever known. The legend of the Seven Sleepers of Ephesus strikingly illustrates the wondrous transformation of society. These Christian brothers, taking shelter in a cave during the Decian persecution, awoke, according to the legend, after a slumber of over a century, to find Christianity everywhere dominant, and a Christian Emperor on the throne of the Cæsars.* The doctrines of Christ, like the rays of the sun, quickly irradiated the world. With choirs and hymns, in cities and villages, in the highways and

---

* Even the sanguine imagination of Tertullian cannot conceive the possibility of this event. " Sed et Cæsares credidissent super Christo," he exclaims, " si aut Cæsares non essent seculo necessario, aut si et Christiani potuis-sent esse Cæsares."—*Apol.*, c. 21.

markets, the praises of the Almighty were sung.
The enemies of God were as though they had not
been.* The Lord brought up the vine of Christianity from a far country, and cast out the
heathen, and planted and watered it, till it twined
round the sceptre of the Cæsars, wreathed the
columns of the Capitol, and filled the whole land.
The heathen fanes were deserted, the gods dis-
crowned, and the pagan flamen no longer offered
sacrifice to the Capitoline Jove.   Rome, which had
dragged so many conquered deities in triumph at
its chariot wheels, at length yielded to a mightier
than all the gods of Olympus. The old faiths
faded from the firmament of human thought as the
stars of midnight at the dawn of day.   The
banished deities forsook their ancient seats. They
walked no longer in the vale of Tempe nor in
the grove of Daphne.   The naiads bathed not in
Scamander's stream nor Simois, nor the nereids
in the waters of the bright Ægean Sea. The
nymphs and dryads ceased to haunt the sylvan
solitudes.   The oriads walked no more in light
on Ida's lofty top.

* Literally, "They are no more because they never
were." Eusebius applies, the promises of Scripture concerning the restoration of the exiled Jews from Babylon
(Psa. lxxx ; xcviii ;) to the condition of Christianity in
his day. The above citations are given in his very words,

O ye vain false gods of Hellas !
Ye are vanished evermore !

Long before the recognition of Christianity as
the religion of the empire, its influence had been
felt permeating the entire community.   Amid the
disintegration of society it was the sole con-
servative element—the salt which preserved it
from corruption.   In the midst of anarchy and
confusion a commuuity was being organized on
a principle previously unknown in the heathen
world, ruling not by terror but by love ; by moral
power, uot by physical force ; inspired by lofty
faith amid a world of unbelief, and cultivating
moral purity amid the reeking abominations of a
sensual age.

We should do scant justice to the blameless
character, simple dignity, and moral purity of the
primitive Christians, if we forgot the thoroughly
effete and corrupt society by which they were
surrounded.   It would seem almost impossible
for the Christian graces to grow in such a fœtid
atmosphere.   Like the snow-white lily springing
in virgin purity from the muddy ooze, they are
more lovely by contrast with the surrounding
pollutions.   Like flowers that deck a sepulchre,
breathing their fragrance amid scenes of corruption and death, are these holy characters, fragrant
with the breath of heaven amid the social rotten-
ness and moral death of their foul environment.

It is difficult to imagine, and impossible to portray, the abominable pollutions of the times. "Society," says Gibbon, "was a rotten, aimless chaos of sensuality." It was a boiling Acheron of seething passions, unhallowed lusts, and tiger thirst for blood, such as never provoked the wrath of Heaven since God drowned the world with water, or destroyed the Cities of the Plain by fire. Only those who have visited the secret museum of Naples, or that house which no woman may enter at Pompeii, and whose paintings no pen may describe; or, who are familiar with the scathing denunciations of popular vices by the Roman satirists and moralists and by the Christian Fathers, can conceive the appalling depravity of the age and nation. St. Paul, in his epistle to the Church among this very people, hints at some features of their exceeding wickedness. It was a shame even to speak of the things which were done by them, but which gifted poets employed their wit to celebrate. A brutalized monster was deified as God, received divine homage,* and beheld all the world at his feet, and the nations trembled at his nod, while the multitude wallowed in a sty of sensuality.

Christianity was to be the new Hercules to

* While yet alive, Domitian was called, "our Lord and God"—*Dominus et Deus noster.*

cleanse this worse than Augean pollution. The pure morals and holy lives of the believers were a perpetual testimony against abounding iniquity, and a living proof of the regenerating power and transforming grace of God. For they themselves, as one of their apologists asserts, "had been reclaimed from ten thousand vices;" and the Apostle, describing some of the vilest characters, exclaims, "such were some of you, but ye are washed, ye are sanctified." They recoiled with the utmost abhorrence from the pollutions of the age, and became indeed "the salt of the earth," the sole moral antiseptic to prevent the total disintegration of society.

Thus amid idolatrous usages and unspeakable moral degradation the Christians lived, a holy nation, a peculiar people. " We alone are without crime," says Tertullian ; " no Christian suffers but for his religion." "Your prisons are full," says Minutius Felix, " but they contain not one Christian." And these holy lives were an argument which even the heathen could not gainsay. The ethics of paganism were the speculations of the cultivated few who aspired to the character of philosophers. The ethics of Christianity were a system of practical duty affecting the daily life of the most lowly and unlettered. "Philosophy," says Lecky, " may dignify, but is impotent to

regenerate man; it may cultivate virtue, but
cannot restrain vice." But Christianity intro-
duced a new sense of sin and of holiness, of
everlasting reward and of endless condemnation.
It planted a sublime, impassioned love of Christ
in the heart, inflaming all its affections. It transformed the character from icy stoicism or epicurean selfishness to a boundless and uncalculating
self-abnegation and devotion.

This divine principle developed a new instinct
of philanthropy in the soul. A feeling of common
brotherhood knit the hearts of the believers
together. To love a slave! to love an enemy! was
accounted the impossible among the heathen;
yet this incredible virtue they beheld every day
among the Christians. "This surprised them
beyond measure," says Tertullian, "that one man
should die for another." Hence, in the Christian
inscriptions no word of bitterness, even toward
their persecutors, is to be found. Sweet peace,
the peace of God that passeth all understanding,
breathes on every side.

One of the most striking results of the new
spirit of philanthropy which Christianity intro-
duced is seen in the copious charity of the
primitive Church. Amid the ruins of ancient
palaces and temples, theatres and baths, there are
none of any house of mercy. Charity among the

pagans, was at best, a fitful and capricious fancy.
Among the Christians it was a vast and vigorous
organization and was cultivated with noble
enthusiasm. And the great and wicked city of
Rome, with its fierce oppressions and inhuman
wrongs, afforded amplest opportunity for the
Christ-like ministrations of love and pity. There
were Christian slaves to succour, exposed to un-
utterable indignities and cruel punishment, even
unto crucifixion for conscience' sake. There were
often martyrs' pangs to assuage, the aching
wounds inflicted by the rack or by the nameless
tortures of the heathen to bind up, and their
bruised and broken hearts to cheer with heavenly
consolation. There were outcast babes to pluck
from death. There were a thousand forms of suffering and sorrow to relieve; and the ever-present
thought of Him who came, not to be ministered
unto, but to minister and to give His life a
ransom for many, was an inspiration to heroic
sacrifice and self-denial. And doubtless the
religion of mercy won its way to many a stony
pagan heart by the winsome spell of the saintly
charities and heavenly benedictions of the persecuted Christians. This sublime principle has
since covered the earth with its institutions of
mercy, and with a passionate zeal has sought out
the woes of man in every land, in order to their
relief.

In the primitive Church voluntary collections*
were regularly made for the poor, the aged, the
sick, the brethren in bonds, and for the burial
of the dead. All fraud and deceit was abhorred,
and all usury forbidden. Many gave all their
goods to feed the poor. "Our charity dispenses
more in the streets," says Tertullian to the
heathen, "than your religion in your temples."
He upbraids them for offering to the gods only
the worn-out and useless, such as is given to
dogs. "How monstrous is it," exclaims the
Alexandrian Clement, "to live in luxury while
so many are in want." "As you would receive,
show mercy," says Chrysostom; "make God your
debtor that you may receive again with usury."
The Church at Antioch, he tells us, maintained
three thousand widows and virgins, besides the
sick and the poor. Under the persecuting Decius
the widows and the infirm under the care of
the Church at Rome were fifteen hundred.
"Behold the treasures of the Church," said St.
Lawrence pointing to the aged and poor, when
the heathen prefect came to confiscate its wealth.
The Church in Carthage sent a sum equal to
four thousand dollars to ransom Christian captives in Numidia. St. Ambrose sold the sacred

* Nemo compellitur, sed sponte confert.—*Tertul.
Apol.* c. 39.

vessels of the Church of Milan to rescue prisoners from the Goths, esteeming it their truest consecration to the service of God. " Better clothe the Christ," says living temples of Jerome, "than adorn the temples of stone." " God has no need of plates and dishes," said Acacius, Bishop of Amida, and he ransomed therewith a number of poor captives. For a similar purpose Paulinus of Nola sold the treasures of his beautiful church, and, it is said, even sold himself into African slavery. The Christian traveller was hospitably entertained by the faithful; and before the close of the fourth century asylums were provided for the sick, aged, and infirm. During the Decian persecution, when the streets of Carthage were strewn with the dying and the dead, the Christians, with the scars of recent torture and imprisonment upon them, exhibited the nobility of a gospel revenge in their care for their fever-smitten persecutors, and seemed to seek the martyrdom of Christian charity, even more glorious than that they had escaped. In the plague of Alexandria, six hundred *parabolani* periled their lives to succour the dying and bury the dead. Julian urged the pagan priests to imitate the virtues of the lowly Christians..

Christianity also gave a new sanctity to human life. The exposure of infants was a fearfully

prevalent pagan practice, which even Plato and
Aristotle permitted. We have had evidences of
the tender charity of the Christians in rescuing
these foundlings from death, or from a fate more
dreadful still—a life of infamy. Christianity
also emphatically affirmed the Almighty's " canon
'gainst self-slaughter," which crime the pagans
had even exalted into a virtue. It taught that a
patient endurance of suffering, like Job's, exhibited a loftier courage than Cato's renunciation
of life.

We have thus seen from the testimony of the
Catacombs, the immense superiority, in all the
elements of true dignity and excellence, of
primitive Christianity to the corrupt civilization
by which it was surrounded. It ennobled the
character and purified the morals of mankind. It
raised society from the ineffable slough into which
it had fallen, imparted tenderness and fidelity to
the domestic relations of life, and enshrined
marriage in a sanctity before unknown. Notwithstanding the corruptions by which it became
infected in the days of its power and pride, even
the worst form of Christianity was infinitely
preferable to the abominations of paganism. It
gave a sacredness before unconceived to human
life. It averted the sword from the throat of the
gladiator, and, plucking helpless infancy from

exposure to untimely death, nourished it in Christian homes. It threw the ægis of its protection over the slave and the oppressed, raising them from the condition of beasts to the dignity of men and the fellowship of saints. With an unwearied and passionate charity it yearned over the suffering and the sorrowing everywhere, and created a vast and comprehensive organization for their relief, of which the world had before no example and had formed no conception. It was a holy Vestal, ministering at the altar of humanity, witnessing ever of the Divine, and keeping the sacred fire burning, not for Rome, but for the world. Its winsome gladness and purity, in an era of unspeakable pollution and sadness, revived the sinking heart of mankind, and made possible a Golden Age in the future transcending far that which poets pictured in the past. It blotted out cruel laws, like those of Draco, written in blood, and led back Justice, long banished, to the judgment seat. It ameliorated the rigours of the penal code, and, as experience has shown, lessened the amount of crime. It created an art purer and loftier than that of paganism; and a literature rivaling in elegance of form, and surpassing in nobleness of spirit, the sublimest productions of the classic muse. Instead of the sensual conceptions of heathenism, polluting the soul, it supplied images of purity, tenderness, and pathos, which fascinated the imagination and hallowed the heart. It taught the sanctity of suffering and of weakness, and the supreme majesty of gentleness and truth.*

NOTE.—The entire subject of Christian evidences from the Catacombs, which has been so cursorily glanced at in the foregoing pages, is treated with great fullness of detail and copious pictorial illustration in a work by the writer, " The Catacombs of Rome, and their Testimony Relative to Primitive Christianity." Cr. 8vo., 560 pp., 136 engravings. New York : Phillips & Hunt. Price $2.50. It discusses at length the structure, origin, and history of the Catacombs ; their art and symbolism; their epigraphy as illustrative of the theology, ministry, rites, and institutions of the primitive Church, and Christian Life and Character in the early ages. The gradual corruption of doctrine and practice and introduction of Romanist errors, as the *cultus* of Mary, the primacy of Peter, prayers of the dead, the invocation of saints, the notion of purgatory, the celibacy of the clergy, rite of monastic orders, and other allied subjects are fully treated.

THE END.

TORONTO:

GUARDIAN OFFICE PRINT, COURT STREET.

OUR PUBLICATIONS.

Works by Rev. John Carroll, D.D.

CASE AND HIS COTEMPORARIES. A Biographical History of Methodism in Canada. 5 vols., cloth, $4.90.

METHODIST BAPTISM. Limp cloth, 15 cents.

FATHER CORSON. Being the Life of the late Rev. Robert Corson. 12mo., cloth, 90 cents

THE EXPOSITION EXPOUNDED, DEFENDED, AND SUPPLEMENTED. Limp cloth, 40 cents.

SCHOOL OF THE PROPHETS; OR, FATHER McROREY'S CLASS AND SQUIRE FIRSTMAN'S KITCHEN FIRE. A Book for Methodists. 264 pages, cloth, 80 cents.

THOUGHTS AND CONCLUSIONS OF A MAN OF YEARS, CONCERNING CHURCHES AND CHURCH CONNECTION. Paper, 5 cents.

Works by W. M. Punshon, D.D., LL.D.

LECTURES AND SERMONS. Printed on thick superfine paper, 378 pages, with a fine steel portrait, and strongly bound in extra fine cloth, $1.

THE PRODIGAL SON, FOUR DISCOURSES ON. 87 pages. Paper cover, 25 cents; cloth, 35 cents.

THE PULPIT AND THE PEW: THEIR DUTIES TO EACH OTHER AND TO GOD. Two Addresses. Paper cover, 10 cents; cloth, 45 cents.

TABOR; OR, THE CLASS-MEETING. A Plea and an Appeal. Paper, 5 cents each; 30 cents per dozen.

CANADA AND ITS RELIGIOUS PROSPECTS. Paper, 5 cents.

MEMORIAL SERMONS. Containing a Sermon, each, by Drs. Punshon, Gervase Smith, J. W. Lindsay, and A. P. Lowrey. Paper, 25 cents; cloth, 35 cents.

Works by Rev. J. Jackson Wray.

NESTLETON MAGNA, A STORY OF YORKSHIRE METHODISM. Illustrated. 12mo., cloth, $1.

MATTHEW MELLOWDEW, A STORY WITH MORE HEROES THAN ONE. Illustrated. 12mo., cloth, $1.

PAUL MEGGITT'S DELUSION. Illustrated. 12mo., cloth, $1.

Works by Rev. W. H. Withrow, D.D.

GREAT PREACHERS. Cloth, 60 cents.

KING'S MESSENGER; or, LAWRENCE TEMPLE'S PROBATION. Cloth, 75 cents.

METHODIST WORTHIES. Cloth, 60 cents.

NEVILLE TRUEMAN, THE PIONEER PREACHER. Cloth, 75 cents.

ROMANCE OF MISSIONS. Cloth, 60 cents.

THE LIQUOR TRAFFIC. Paper, 5 cents.

PROHIBITION, THE DUTY OF THE HOUR. Paper, 5 cents.

IS ALCOHOL FOOD? Paper, 5 cents.

THE BIBLE AND THE TEMPERANCE QUESTION. Paper, 10 cents.

THE PHYSIOLOGICAL EFFECTS OF ALCOHOL. Paper, 10 cents.

INTEMPERANCE; ITS EVILS AND THEIR REMEDIES. Paper, 15 cents.

In Press,

POPULAR HISTORY OF CANADA. 600 pp., 8vo. Five steel engravings and 100 woodcuts.

Works by John Ashworth.

STRANGE TALES FROM HUMBLE LIFE. First Series, cloth, $1.

STRANGE TALES FROM HUMBLE LIFE. Second Series, cloth, 45 cents.

Works by Rev. J. Cynddylan Jones.

STUDIES IN MATTHEW. 12mo., cloth, $1.25.

STUDIES IN THE ACTS. 12mo., cloth, $1.50.

In preparation by the same Author.

STUDIES IN THE GOSPEL ACCOLDING TO ST. JOHN.

WESLEY'S DOCTRINAL STANDARDS. Part I. The Sermons, with Introductions, Analysis, and Notes. By Rev. N. Burwash, S.T.D. Prof. of Theology in the University of Victoria College, Cobourg. Large 8vo., cloth, 536 pages, $2.50.

ARROWS IN THE HEART OF THE KING'S ENEMIES; or, ATHEISTIC ERRORS OF THE DAY REFUTED, AND THE DOCTRINE OF A PERSONAL GOD VINDICATED. By the Rev. Alexander W. McLeod, D.D., at one time editor of the *Wesleyan*, Halifax, N.S., now a minister of the M.E. Church, Baltimore, U.S. 12mo, cloth, 128 pages. 45 cents.

SPIRITUAL STRUGGLES OF A ROMAN CATHOLIC. An Autobiographical Sketch. By Louis N. Beaudry, with an introduction by Rev. B. Hawley, D.D. With steel portrait. Cloth, $1.00.

THE RELIGION OF LIFE; OR CHRIST AND NICODEMUS. By John G. Manly. Cloth, 50 cents.

CYCLOPÆDIA OF METHODISM IN CANADA. Containing Historical, Educational, and Statistical Information, dating from the beginning of the work in the several Provinces in the Dominion of Canada. By Rev. George H. Cornish. With artotype portrait. 8vo., cloth, $4.50; sheep, $5.

LOYALISTS OF AMERICA AND THEIR TIMES. By Rev. Egerton Ryerson, LL.D. 2 vols., large 8vo., with portrait. Cloth, $5; half morocco, $7.

COMPANION TO THE REVISED NEW TESTAMENT. By Alex. Roberts, D.D.; and an American Revisor. Paper, 30 cents; cloth, 65 cents.

LIFE OF HON. JUDGE WILMOT. By Rev. J. Lathern. With artotype portrait. 12mo., cloth, 75 cents.

LIFE OF J. B. MORROW. By Rev. A. W. Nicolson. 75 cents.

LIFE OF GIDEON OUSELY. By Rev. William Arthur, M.A. Cloth, $1.

OLD CHRISTIANITY AGAINST PAPAL NOVELTIES. By Gideon Ouseley. Illustrated. Cloth, $1.

A SUMMER IN PRAIRIE-LAND. By Rev. Alexander Sutherland, D.D. Illustrated. 12mo., paper, 40 cents; cloth, 70 cents.

LIFE AND TIMES OF ANSON GREEN, D.D. Written by himself. 12mo., cloth, with portrait, $1.

VOICES FROM THE THRONE; OR, GOD'S CALLS TO FAITH AND OBEDIENCE. By Rev. J. C. Seymour. Cloth, 50 cents.

THE GUIDING ANGEL. By Kate Murray. 18mo., cloth, 30 cents.

LONE LAND LIGHTS. By Rev. J. McLean. Cloth, extra, 12mo., 75 pages, 35 cent..

APPLIED LOGIC. By S. S. Nelles, LL.D. Cloth, 75 cents.

CHRISTIAN REWARDS. By Rev. J. S. Evans. Cloth, 50 cents.

CHRISTIAN PERFECTION. By Rev. J. Wesley. Paper, 10 cents; cloth, 20 cents.

THE CLASS-LEADER: HIS WORK AND HOW TO DO IT. By J. Atkinson, M.A. Cloth, 60 cents.

CONVERSATIONS ON BAPTISM. By Rev. A. Langford. Cloth, 30 cents.

CATECHISM OF BAPTISM. By D. D. Currie. Cloth, 50 cents.

SERMONS ON CHRISTIAN LIFE. By Rev. C. W. Hawkins. 12mo., cloth, $1.

MEMORIALS OF MR. AND MRS. JACKSON. With steel portrait. Cloth, 75 cents.

CIRCUIT REGISTER. $1.50.

WEEKLY OFFERING BOOK. $1.50.

DISCIPLINE OF THE METHODIST CHURCH OF CANADA. 60 cents.

METHODIST HYMN-BOOK. In various sizes and styles of binding. Prices from 30 cents upwards.

METHODIST CATECHISMS. No. I, per dozen, 25 cents. No. II, per dozen, 60 cents. No. III, per dozen, 75 cents.

SUNDAY-SCHOOL RECORD BOOK. $1.25.

SUNDAY-SCHOOL MINUTE BOOK. Designed by Thomas Wallis. 60 cts.

SUNDAY-SCHOOL REGISTER. 50 cents.

SECRETARY'S MINUTE BOOK. 50 cents.

LIBRARIAN'S ACCOUNT BOOK. 50 cents.

THE TEMPERANCE BATTLE-FIELD, AND HOW TO GAIN THE DAY. By Rev. J. C. Seymour. 12mo., cloth, 65 cents.

THE NEED OF THE WORLD. By Rev. S. G. Phillips. 12mo, cloth, $1.00.

TOWARD THE SUNRISE. Being Sketches of Travel in Europe and the East. By Rev. Hugh Johnston, M.A.. B.D. 12mo, cloth, illustrated, $1.25.

CANADIAN METHODISM : ITS EPOCHS AND CHARACTERISTS. By the Rev. Egerton Ryerson, D.D., LL.D., author. 12mo. 440 pages. Price, $1.25.

CONSECRATED WOMEN. By M. P. Hack. 12mo, cloth, $1.50.

LIFE OF RICHARD COBDEN. By J. Morley 8vo., cloth, 640 pages, with Portrait, $3.50. The subject of this memoir is the great English liberal, statesman, and orator, the champion of Free Trade, and one of the most prominent agitators for the Repeal of the Corn Laws. He and John Bright have been life-long friends, and his history, like Bright's, is very much the history of the English politics of this century. "To John Bright these memories of his close comrade in the cause of wise, just, and sedate government," the book is inscribed by Mr. Morley, who will be remembered as the author of several successful biographical works, and editor of the "English Men of Letters' series." The material of this biography was supplied by Mr. Cobden's many friends and correspondence.
Mailed, post-free, on receipt of price. ☞ Agents wanted.

LIFE AND SPEECHES OF HON. JOHN BRIGHT. By G. Barnet Smith, Author of the Life of Hon. W. E. Gladstone. Price $1.75. The English Edition sells at Twenty-four Shillings, sterling. One large Crown 8vo. volume of 700 pages, with two fine steel portraits, one from the latest taken of Mr. Bright, the other from a painting made of him in early life.

and his history, like Bright's, is very much the history of the English politics of this century. "To John Bright these memories of his close comrade in the cause of wise, just, and sedate government," the book is inscribed by Mr. Morley, who will be remembered as the author of several successful biographical works, and editor of the "English Men of Letters' series." The material of this biography was supplied by Mr. Cobden's many friends and correspondence.

Mailed, post-free, on receipt of price. ☞ Agents wanted.

LIFE AND SPEECHES OF HON. JOHN BRIGHT. By G. Barnet Smith, Author of the Life of Hon. W. E. Gladstone. Price $1.75. The English Edition sells at Twenty-four Shillings, sterling. One large Crown 8vo. volume of 700 pages, with two fine steel portraits, one from the latest taken of Mr. Bright, the other from a painting made of him in early life.

CHAMBERS' ENCYCLOPÆDIA. Latest edition. Cloth or leather.

ENGLISH DICTIONARIES. Webster and Worcester, Unabridged with new Supplements.

Works on Baptism.

CONVERSATIONS ON BAPTISM. By Rev. Alexander Langford. 16mo., cloth. 30 cents.

CHRISTIC AND PATRISTIC BAPTISM. By J. W. Dale, D.D, 8vo., cloth, $5.

CLASSIC BAPTISM. By J. W. Dale, D.D. 8vo., cloth $3.50.

PÆDOBAPTISTS' GUIDE ON MODE, AND SUBJECT, AND BAPTISMAL REGENERATION. By John Guthrie, M.A. 18mo., cloth, 60 cts.

CHRISTIAN BAPTISM, ITS SUBJECTS AND MODE. By S. M. Merrill, D.D. 12mo., cloth, $1.25.

BAPTISMA, EXEGETICAL AND CONTROVERSIAL. By Rev. J. Lathern. 12mo. cloth. 75 cents.

CATECHISM OF BAPTISM. By Rev. D.D. Currie. 12mo, cloth· 50 cents.

IMMERSION PROVED TO BE NOT A SCRIPTURAL MODE OF BAPTISM but a Romish invention, and Immersionists shown to be disregarding Divine authority in refusing Baptism to the Infant Children of Believers. Paper, 20 cents.

BAPTISM. A New and Important Contribution on this subject by a Southern Minister, Rev. S. Ditzler, D.D., of Louisville, Kentucky, 12mo., cloth. $2.00.

BAPTISM IN A NUTSHELL. Just the Book for Young People. By Rev. M. W. Gifford. Price, postpaid, 15 cents.

A COMPEND OF BAPTISM. By William Hamilton, D.D. Limp cloth, 75 cents ; cloth boards, $1.00.

Works on Plymouth-Brethrenism.

PLYMOUTH-BRETHRENISM. A Refutation of its Principles and Doctrines. By Rev. Thos. Croskerry. 12mo., cloth, 90 cents.

PLYMOUTH-BRETHRENISM UNVEILED AND REFUTED. By Wm. Reid, D.D. 12mo, cloth, 90 cents.

MISLEADING LIGHTS. A Review of Current Antinomian Theories of the Atonement and Justification. By Rev. E. H. Dewart, D.D. Price 3 cents.

BRETHRENISM ; OR THE SPECIAL TEACHINGS, ECCLESIASTICAL AND Doctrinal, of Brethren, or Plymouth-Brethren, compiled from their own writings, with Strictures. By the Rev. Duncan Macintosh. Price 10 cents.

PERIODICALS.

PER YEAR—POSTAGE FREE.

CHRISTIAN GUARDIAN. Weekly. $2.00.

METHODIST MAGAZINE, 96 pages, Monthly. Illustrated. $2.00.

SUNDAY-SCHOOL BANNER, 32 pages, 8vo., Monthly. Under six copies, 65 cents ; over six copies. 60 cents.

CANADIAN SCHOLAR'S QUARTERLY. 8 cents.

QUARTERLY REVIEW SERVICE. By the year, 24 cents a dozen, or $2.00 per 100 ; per quarter, 6 cents a dozen ; 50 cents per 100.

PLEASANT HOURS. 8 pages, 4to., semi-monthly. Single copies, 30 cents ; less than 20 copies, 22 cents ; over 500 copies, 20 cents.

BEREAN LEAVES. Monthly ; 100 copies per month, $5.50.

SUNBEAM. Semi-monthly ; less than 20 copies, 15 cents ; 20 copies and upwards, 12 cents.

HYMN-BOOKS.

8vo, or Pulpit Size, Pica Type, Leaded.

Persian Morocco, gilt edges	$4 00
Morocco, gilt edges	5 00

12mo., or Old People's Size, Pica Type.

Cloth, sprinkled edges	$1 50
Roan, sprinkled edges	2 00
Morocco, gilt edges	3 50
Morocco, extra gilt, gilt edges	4 25

18mo, Small Pica Type.

Cloth, sprinkled edges	0 80
Roan, sprinkled edges	1 10
French Morocco, red edges	1 25
French Morocco, limp, gilt edges	1 40
French Morocco, boards, gilt edges	1 50
Morocco, limp, gilt edges	1 80
Morocco, boards, gilt edges	2 00
Calf, marble edges	2 00
Morocco, extra, gilt edges	2 50

24mo, Brevier Type.

Cloth, sprinkled edges	0 50
Roan, sprinkled edges	0 80
French Morocco, limp	1 00
French Morocco, boards	1 10
Morocco, gilt edges	1 50

Small Flat 32mo, Pearl Type.

Cloth, sprinkled edges	0 30
Roan, sprinkled edges	0.45
French Morocco, gilt edges	0 70
Morocco, limp, gilt edges	1 00
Morocco, boards, gilt edges	1 10
Morocco, extra gilt, gilt edges	1 50

Large Flat Crown 8vo, Brevier Type.

Cloth, sprinkled edges	0 60
Roan, sprinkled edges	0 90
French Morocco, limp, gilt edges	1 20
French Morocco, boards, gilt edges	1 25
Morocco, limp, gilt edges	1 75
Morocco, extra gilt, gilt edges	2 25
Levant Morocco, limp, kid lined, yapped, gilt edges	2 75

THE BIBLE AND METHODIST HYMN-BOOK COMBINED. The sheets of the Bible are printed in ruby type, and have been imported from England especially for this purpose, as well as the paper on which the Hymns are printed. 32mo., full morocco circuit, gilt edges, $3.50, French Morocco, boards, gilt edges, $1.75.

BIBLE AND METHODIST HYMN-BOOK. Larger size and type than the above. The Bible is printed in minion type, and the Hymns in brevier on English paper. Crown 8vo., morocco circuit, gilt edges, $5.00. Levant morocco, kid lined, gilt edges, $6.00.

OUR
Music Book Department.

Church Music Books.

	Each.	Per Doz.
Methodist Tune-Book, Cloth	1 00	10 00
" " Leather	1 50	15 00
Bristol Tune Book	$1 20	$12 00
Gospel Praise Book	0 40	4 00
Canadian Church Harmonist	1 00	10 00
Chapel Anthem	1 25	12 00
Canadian Anthem Book	1 25	12 00
Dominion Singer (Harp and Organ)	0 90	9 00
Temple Anthems	1 25	12 00
Gospel Male Choir	0 60	6 00
Congregational Anthems	0 75	7 20
Royal Anthems	1 25	12 00
Palmer's Anthems	1 00	10 00

Singing Schools, Conventions, etc., Music Books.

	Each.	Per Doz.
Song Leader	0 75	7 50
Sovereign	0 75	7 50
Vineyard of Song	0 75	
Choice	0 75	

Sabbath-School Music Books.

	Each.	Per Doz.
Sabbath-school Wave, board Covers	0 50	5 00
" Organ, "	0 50	5 00
" Harp, "	0 40	4 00
" Harmonium, "	0 35	3 60
Royal Gems, "	0 35	3 60
Shining Strand,	0 20	1 80

OUR PUBLICATIONS.

			Each.	Per Doz.
Gems of Gospel Song,	Board Covers	....	0 35	$4 20
Redeemer's Praise,	"	....	0 35	3 60
Gem of Gems,	"	....	0 35	3 60
Heart and Voice,	"	....	0 35	3 60
Joy and Gladness,	"	....	0 35	3 60
Welcome Tidings,	"	....	0 35	3 60
Wreath of Praise,	"	....	0 35	3 60
Jasper and Gold,	"	....	0 35	3 60
White Robes,	"	....	0 35	8 60
The Hymnary,	"	....	0 50	5 00
Brightest and Best,	"	....	0 35	3 60
The New Song,	"	....	0 50	5 40
New Joy Bells,	"	....	0 35	3 60
Crystal Songs,	"	....	0 35	3 60
Winnowed Hymns,	' "	....	0 30	3 00
Crown of Life,	"	....	0 35	3 60
Songs and Solos. Enlarged.	Paper covers	....	0 30	3 00
" " "	Cloth "	....	0 45	4 80
Songs of Love and Mercy.	Paper "	....	0 30	3 00
" " "	Cloth "	....	0 45	4 80
Joy to the World.	Board "	....	0 35	3 60
Good as Gold,	" "	....	0 35	3 60
Gospel Hymns & Sacred Songs	" "	....	0 35	3 60
" " " " 1, 2, & 3, Cloth covers			1 00	10 00
" " " " No. 4, Board "			0 35	3 60
" " " " " Paper "			0 30	3 00
Gospel Hymns, Combined Ed. with No. 4. Boards ..			1 00	10 00
" " " " " Cloth ..			1 25	12 00

Temperance Music Books.

Temperance Jewels	....		0 35	3 60

Companion, or Words Only.

			Each.	Per Doz.
Sabbath-school Wave	....		0 15	1 20
" Organ	....		0 15	1 75
" Harmonium	....		0 15	1 20
Harp and Organ in One	....		0 30	3 00
Songs and Solos. Enlarged.	Paper covers	......	0 05	0 60
" " "	Cloth "	......	0 10	0 90
Songs of Love and Mercy.	Paper "	......	0 05	0 60
" " "	Cloth "	......	0 10	0 90
Gospel Hymns & Sacred Songs.	Paper "	....	0 05	0 48
" " " "	Cloth "	......	0 07	0 60
" " " " 1, 2 & 3, Cloth covers..			0 20	2 00
" " " " 1,2,3,& 4, " ..			0 25	2 50
" " " " 1,2,3.& 4, B'd covers..			0 20	2 00
" " " " No. 4. Paper " ..			0 05	0 48

SUNDAY-SCHOOL LIBRARIES

It will be to your advantage, if you want good, sound, Sunday-School Library Books, to write for lists. Our Libraries are cheap.

Dominion Libraries.

No. 1, 50 volumes, 16mo. ....$25 60 net.
No. 2, 100   "   18mo. .... 25 00 "

Little People's Picture Library.

50 volumes, 48mo......................................$10 00 net.

Acme Libraries.

No. 1, 50 volumes, 16mo. ....$25 00 net
No. 2, 50   "   16mo. .... 25 00 "

Excelsior Libraries.

No. 1, 50 volumes, 18mo. ....$15 00 net
No. 2, 40   "   18mo. .... 14 00 "
No. 3, 15   "   12mo. .... 9 00 "
No. 4, 15   "   12mo. .... 9 00 "

Model Libraries.

No. 1, 50 volumes, 16mo. ....$22 00 net.
No. 2, 50   "   18mo. .... 16 50 "
No. 3, 50   "   16mo. .... 27 50 "

Economical Libraries.

No. A, 50 volumes, 12mo..............................$24 50 net.
No. B, 50   "   12mo........................... 29 0 "
No. C, 40   "   12mo........................... 18 50 "

Primary Library.

40 volumes, 18mo......................................$7 50 net.

The Olive Library.

40 large 16mo. volumes ....$25 00 net.

TORONTO SELECTED LIBRARIES.

No. 1, 100 volumes, 16mo.................................$25 00
No. 2, 100   "   16mo................................. 25 00
No. 5, 100   "   16mo................................. 25 00

All the above-mentioned Library Books contain many illustrations, are strongly bound, and put up in neat boxes ready for shipping. These Libraries are giving great satisfaction wherever sold.

Be sure to send for Lists of the Books contained in these Libraries, also of

SUNDAY-SCHOOL REQUISITES,

of which we have a large variety, to

WILLIAM BRIGGS;

78 & 80 King Street East, Toronto.

CLERGYMEN'S AND STUDENTS' HEALTH ; OR, THE TRUE WAY TO ENJOY LIFE. By W. M. Cornell, M.D. 12mo., cloth, 300 pp., $1.15.

DRILL BOOK IN VOCAL CULTURE AND GESTURE. By Professor E. P. Thwing. Fifth edition. 12mo., manilla, 115 pp., 25c.*

FULTON'S REPLIES TO BEECHER, FARRAR, AND INGERSOLL ON HELL. Three Sermons. One vol., 8vo., paper, 38 pp., 10c.*

GILEAD ; OR, THE VISION OF ALL SOULS' HOSPITAL. An Allegory. By Rev. J. Hyatt Smith, Member of Congress elect. 12mo., 360 pp., $1.15.

HANDBOOK OF ILLUSTRATIONS. By Rev. E. P. Thwing. First Series. Third edition. 25c.* Second Series, Just issued, 25c.*

HOME ALTAR. By Dr. Deems. New edition. 12mo., Cloth, 281 pp., 90c.

THE HOMILIST. By David Thomas, D.D. Vol. XII., Editor's Series. Cloth, 12mo., 368 pp., heavy tinted paper, $1.50.

HOMILETIC ENCYCLOPÆDIA OF ILLUSTRATIONS IN THEOLOGY AND MORALS. A Handbook of Practical Divinity, and a Commentary on Holy Scripture. By Rev. R. A. Bertram. Royal 8vo., cloth, 892 pp., $4.50.

HOW TO PAY CHURCH DEBTS. By Sylvanus Stall. It is the only book on this subject. 12mo., 280 pp., tinted paper, $1.75.

GODET'S COMMENTARY ON THE GOSPEL OF ST. LUKE. With Preface and Notes. By John Hall, D.D. $2.80.

THESE SAYINGS OF MINE. By Jos. Parker, D.D. 8vo., cloth, heavy paper, $1.75.

THINGS NEW AND OLD. A Storehouse of Illustrations, Apologues, Adages, with their several applications, collected from the writings and sayings of the learned in all ages. By John Spencer. To which is added, "A Treasury of Smiles," by Robert Cawdray. Royal 8vo., cloth, over 1,100 pp., $4.80.

STANDARD SERIES. CLASS A. Fifteen volumes by the most Eminent Authors. Nos. 1, 2, 5, 6, 7, 9, 10, 11, 20, 21, 32, 40, 41, 42, and 43 of Standard Series, bound in one vol. 4to., cloth, 670 pp., $3.50.

POPULAR HISTORY OF ENGLAND, By Charles Knight. 4to., 1,370 pp. Bound handsomely in cloth, 2 vols., $3.75.

☞ *Books marked with a * are sold net.*

Standard Series of cheap books bound in manilla. From Nos. 1 to 67, now ready. Prices vary.

☞ Send for Catalogue giving a complete list of our miscellaneous books.

All the latest leading books received, and kept in stock as soon as published.

TRACTS JUST PUBLISHED.

UNIVERSAL CHILDHOOD DRAWN TO CHRIST: WITH AN APPENDIX CONTAINING REMARKS ON REV. DR. BURWASH'S "MORAL CONDITION OF CHILDHOOD." By H. F. BLAND. Paper, 10 cents.

THE RELATION OF CHILDREN TO THE FALL, THE ATONEMENT, AND THE CHURCH. By N. BURWASH, S.T.D. Paper, 15 cents.

SALVATION OF INFANTS; OR, A WORD OF COMFORT TO BEREAVED CHRISTIAN PARENTS. By the Rev. W. A. McKAY, B.A. Paper, 10 cents.

IMMERSION PROVED TO BE NOT A SCRIPTURAL MODE OF BAPTISM BUT A ROMISH INVENTION; AND IMMERSIONISTS SHOWN TO BE DISREGARDING DIVINE AUTHORITY IN REFUSING BAPTISM TO THE INFANT CHILDREN OF BELIEVERS. By the Rev. W. A. McKAY, B.A. Paper, 20 cents.

BAPTISM IMPROVED; OR, PARENTS AND CHILDREN SOLEMNLY REMINDED OF THEIR OBLIGATIONS. By the Rev W. A. McKAY, B.A. Paper, 10 cents.

BURIAL IN BAPTISM; a Colloquy, in which the Claims of Ritual Baptism in Romans vi. 3, 4, Colossians ii. 12, are examined, and shown to be Visionary. By the Rev. T. L. WILKINSON. Paper, 5 cents.

THE EVANGELICAL DENOMINATIONS OF THE AGE. By the Rev. S. G. PHILLIPS, M.A. Paper, 15 cents.

THE CLASS MEETING: ITS SCRIPTURAL AUTHORITY AND PRACTICAL VALUE. By the Rev. J. A. CHAPMAN, M.A. Paper, 10 cents.

POPULAR AMUSEMENTS. The duty of the Officers and Members of the Methodist Church in relation thereto. By the Rev. H. KENNER. Paper, 10 cents.

CERTAINTIES IN RELIGION. By the Rev. J. A. WILLIAMS, D.D., F.T.L.; and THE SOUL'S ANCHOR. By the Rev. GEORGE McRITCHIE. Being the Fifth Annual Lecture and Sermon before the Theological Union of Victoria College, in 1882. Paper, 20 cents, net.

ADDRESS,

WILLIAM BRIGGS,

8 & 80 King St. East, TORONTO.